"I stopped Amanda from taking it as far as she wanted to go. I suddenly decided that it was a huge mistake and was about to ask her to leave when she looked out the window and saw the attack."

"She called you over to the window, but you couldn't see anything because your contacts were already out by then," Elizabeth added.

"Exactly," Winston said, his eyes meeting hers. "You know, Liz—I wanted to report it right away, but Amanda's the one who stopped me. She was afraid that if we called the cops, everyone would find out that we'd been together. You see my dilemma, don't you?"

Elizabeth's face grew hot. "I see your dilemma, Winston, but it's still no excuse. That guy almost killed me! You've made one bad decision after another, and people are dying because of it!"

Winston cringed. "I didn't mean to hurt anyone!"

"I don't care what your intentions were; you have to take responsibility for what you've done!" Elizabeth was seething, her eyes glowing fiercely. "Next time this guy strikes, the victim could be Denise," she shouted, heading for the door. "And she might not be as lucky as I was!"

Bantam Books in the Sweet Valley University series.
Ask your bookseller for the books you have missed.

And don't miss these Sweet Valley
University Thriller Editions:

SWEET VALLEY UNIVERSITY®

THRILLER EDITION

What Winston Saw

Written by
Laurie John

Created by
FRANCINE PASCAL

BANTAM BOOKS
NEW YORK · TORONTO · LONDON · SYDNEY · AUCKLAND

RL 6, age 12 and up

WHAT WINSTON SAW

A Bantam Book / January 1997

Sweet Valley High® *and Sweet Valley University*®
are registered trademarks of Francine Pascal.
Conceived by Francine Pascal.
Produced by Daniel Weiss Associates, Inc.
33 West 17th Street
New York, NY 10011.

ISBN: 0-553-57050-1

Published simultaneously in the United States and Canada

Bantam Books are published by Bantam Books, a division of Bantam
Doubleday Dell Publishing Group, Inc. Its trademark, consisting of the
words "Bantam Books" and the portrayal of a rooster, is Registered in
U.S. Patent and Trademark Office and in other countries. Marca
Registrada. Bantam Books, 1540 Broadway, New York, New York 10036.

PRINTED IN THE UNITED STATES OF AMERICA

OPM   0 9 8 7 6 5 4 3 2 1

To Pat Troy

Chapter One

"Where are you, Denise?" Winston Egbert slammed down the telephone receiver and let out a loud, frustrated grunt. He rocked impatiently in his office chair, dark brown eyes fixed on the large framed photo of his girlfriend on the corner of the desk. Denise's beautiful, sunlit features smiled back at him wordlessly.

Winston picked up the photo and caressed the glossy wooden frame with the tip of his fingers. For the past week Denise been house-sitting for her aunt, who was vacationing in Hawaii. Denise was staying at the beach house every night and commuted to school in the mornings, and for some reason she was incredibly hard to reach. Even though the beach house was only fifteen miles from campus, to Winston it might as well have been far away in the wilds of Siberia.

Call me, Denise, Winston pleaded under his breath. His chest caved in as he gazed at her smooth, shoulder-length curls. *I miss you.*

"Winston, are you listening to me?"

Snapping to attention, Winston tore his eyes away from the photo to see Dean Franklin's perfectly tailored three-piece suit towering above him. Winston cleared his throat. "I'm sorry, sir," he said, tripping over his words. "I guess I just spaced out a little." He thumbed through the nearest file folder in a lame attempt to look busy.

The dean smiled, making tiny wrinkles appear near his graying temples. "My wife is here to take me out to lunch," he said, gesturing to the open door of his office. "Amanda, this is my new assistant, Winston Egbert."

Winston had imagined Mrs. John Franklin to be a distinguished, middle-aged woman, but instead he was blown away by the sight of a curvy knockout with long blond hair who was waving to him from across the room. *He did say wife, didn't he?* She had to be at least twenty years younger than the dean.

"Nice to meet you, uh . . . Mrs. Franklin," Winston squeaked.

Mrs. Franklin smiled warmly. "Please, Winston, call me Amanda."

"OK . . . Amanda." Realizing that he was staring, Winston turned his attention back to his boss. *Way to go, Dean Franklin,* Winston mused to himself.

A faint, sly grin crossed the dean's lips for a split second, as if even *he* couldn't believe his good fortune. "Whoever calls, tell them I'll be back by three o'clock," he instructed. "You can either take a message or put them through to my voice mail."

Winston reached for a pink message pad. "Got it."

"If there's an emergency, I can be reached at Da Vinci's Restaurant—but I don't expect there'll be any problems." Dean Franklin turned around and looked at his wife, who was smoothing down the front of her unbelievably short red skirt. "I have to make one quick phone call, sweetheart, then we can go."

"Of course," Amanda purred.

As soon as the dean went back into his office Winston returned his attention to the photograph of Denise. If he didn't talk to her soon, he was pretty sure he was going to go crazy. *Maybe she went back to her dorm room for something,* Winston suddenly thought. He dialed the number.

Four rings, then a click. "Hey, this is Denise. Leave me a message—and oh yeah, don't forget to recycle. The planet you save might be your own. Have a nice day."

Winston spouted off his message without

even waiting for the beep. "I would love to have a nice day, Denise, but I'm feeling pretty miserable because I can't seem to track you down. Aren't we supposed to go to your sorority party tonight? What's going on? Call me as soon as you can. I miss you. Call me." Winston hung up the phone and gasped for air, having run through the entire message in a single breath.

"Making personal calls at work, Mr. Egbert?"

Startled, Winston dropped the receiver and spun around in his chair. The dean's wife stood in the doorway, arms folded in front of her, one perfectly shaped eyebrow arched in disapproval.

Winston's face burned red. *Good going, Egbert. The boss's wife thinks you're a slacker,* he thought miserably. Fifty students had applied for the work-study job in the dean's office, and somehow Winston had managed to snag it. That meant that there were still forty-nine eager students just waiting for Winston to mess up so one of them could replace him. Winston decided he'd have to do some serious backpedaling to get on Amanda's good side or else he could kiss the job good-bye.

"Amanda—hi . . . I, uh, just had to give my girlfriend a quick call," Winston stammered as he ran a nervous hand through his thick brown hair. A series of sparks ignited in his brain like firecrackers as he rapidly formulated the perfect excuse. "She's, uh, sick with the flu. She's been in bed all day."

Amanda strode over to Winston's desk, her high heels clicking ominously against the cool floor tiles. A look of skepticism remained on her perfect features. "If she's been in bed all day, how come you left a message on her machine?"

Winston swallowed a gulp of thick air. If goofing off at work wasn't reason enough to get him fired, getting caught in a lie would certainly do it. He had to come clean.

"You're right, Mrs. Franklin—I mean, Amanda. I'm sorry. I shouldn't have used the phone during work," Winston said. He bowed his head.

The honest approach seemed to work because Amanda Franklin's soft mouth curved into a slow grin. She turned around and gracefully balanced herself against the edge of Winston's desk. "Whatever you want to do, Winston, it doesn't matter to me," she said in a velvety whisper. Her brown eyes shot a glance in the dean's direction. "*He's* the one you're working for."

"I'll try to be more careful," Winston insisted. The confidential tone of Amanda's voice put him at ease. It was clear that she had no intention of telling the dean about Winston's error in judgment. His shoulders sagged with relief. *Maybe I'll be able to keep the job after all.*

Amanda picked up the framed photograph of Denise. A clean, peachy scent filled the air as she moved. "Is this your girlfriend?"

Winston nodded. "Her name is Denise."

"Pretty name," Amanda answered, setting the frame back on the desk. "Have you two been together long?"

Winston leaned back in his chair and inhaled deeply. "Yeah, for quite a while. We live in the same dorm."

"That's sweet." Amanda brushed her wavy, ash blond hair over one shoulder and crossed her legs. "But is everything going OK? I couldn't help overhearing your message. You sounded upset about something."

"I—I wasn't that upset," Winston answered distractedly, becoming more and more aware of the close proximity of Amanda's long, curvy legs. "Sometimes she's just not home when I call."

"Let me tell you something, Winston," Amanda said with a playful laugh. She put a well-manicured hand on Winston's shoulder and slowly let it slide toward his chest. "If *I* were your girlfriend, I'd be sure to be home when you called."

A damp heat smoldered under Winston's Sweet Valley University sweatshirt, just below the place where Amanda's hand rested. *Is she flirting with me, or am I imagining this?* Winston

6

blinked a few times to make sure. Amanda was gorgeous and sophisticated—hardly the kind of woman who could be interested in him. All his life Winston had been known as the goofball or the class clown. Beautiful, sexy women just didn't throw themselves at his size-twelve feet. Denise was the only exception, and even Winston knew that a guy like him could never be so lucky twice in one lifetime.

Unless, of course, a mystical force of nature were involved.

Or maybe it's my new contact lenses, Winston mused, sitting up straight in his chair. He flashed Amanda a blinding smile.

"Ready to go, honey?" the dean called from his office.

"Coming," Amanda answered sweetly. She walked behind Winston, running her fingers lightly along the back of his chair. "It was nice meeting you, Winston. I'm sure we'll cross paths again."

Winston nodded, watching Amanda's hourglass figure as she walked out the door. "I'm sure we will."

Denise Waters made her way over to the tight circle of her impeccably dressed sorority sisters who had gathered in the middle of the crowded Theta parlor. It was the semiannual Theta Sorority and Sigma Fraternity midterm bash, a celebration before exams kicked in—but really it was just an excuse for a party. Denise automatically clicked her fingers to the raging beat of the dance music, but she wasn't really in the mood to kick up her heels and have a good time. There was too much on her mind.

"So I said to the guy, 'Excuse me, there's no way that's a real Chanel suit—the buttons are *plastic!*'" Jessica Wakefield tossed her long blond hair over one shoulder, captivating her audience with another one of her famous shopping stories. The blue-green sheath she was wearing not only showed off her trim figure but brought out the color of her aquamarine eyes as well.

"What did he say?" Isabella Ricci asked, nibbling on a canapé.

Jessica gave the group a sly look. "He said he'd sell it to me for fifty."

"No way!" the group said with a collective murmur. Denise poured herself a glass of sparkling water.

"But I didn't take it," Jessica went on. "I badgered the poor guy until he practically begged me to buy it for twenty-five."

Isabella clapped. "You are a shopping genius, my dear. I wish Lila was here—she'd really appreciate a good story like that."

"She's spending a week in Paris," Jessica reminded them. "I'm sure she's making shopping history all on her own."

"Speaking of Lila, it looks like her better half just walked through the door," Isabella said.

"You mean *worse* half," Jessica muttered.

Denise's eyes were immediately drawn to the front door, where Lila Fowler's boyfriend, Bruce Patman, had just walked in. He was president of the Sigmas, with a strong, chiseled jaw and strikingly handsome face, thick, dark hair, and broad, muscular shoulders. He was charming and confident—perhaps *too* confident by some people's standards, but Denise often thought he was judged too harshly. Not everyone knew about Bruce's sweet, romantic side.

I'm so glad you're here, Denise thought, feeling a bit of tension melting away. *One less thing to worry about.*

Denise excused herself from the group and wove her petite frame through the towering group of Greeks who were swarming around their president. Bruce grinned broadly, like a movie star on his way to the Academy Awards.

Making a tight squeeze through the group, Denise finally reached him. "Bruce, I need to talk to you before Winston gets here," she said above the noise of the crowd. "Can you meet me in the kitchen?"

Bruce snagged a mini–egg roll from one of the gleaming silver trays and popped it into his

9

mouth. "Anything for you, Denise," he said with a wink.

She took his hand and led him down the side hallway to the kitchen. "I was afraid Winston was going to get here before you. That would've been a mess."

"Sorry—I like to make an entrance." Bruce was leaning against the counter. "Nice dress, by the way."

"Thanks," Denise said modestly, looking down at the simple black evening gown she'd borrowed from her aunt's closet. "It's my aunt's—I'm house-sitting for her while she's in Hawaii."

"At the beach house?"

Denise nodded. "Look, Bruce, we don't have much time before Winston gets here." She felt her face reddening. "Have you given any thought to what I asked you Saturday night?"

Bruce's face grew serious. "I have—and I think it's a good idea."

He said yes! Denise wanted to jump for joy, but she contained herself. Suddenly someone shouted from the parlor, "Hey, Winston! How are you doing, buddy?"

Denise and Bruce exchanged looks. The burst of excitement she felt rapidly deteriorated. "Great timing," she said with a sigh. "Can you hang on for a second? I'll be right back."

She darted into the hallway and caught

10

Winston by the door. "There you are," Winston said, smiling weakly. He wrapped his arm around her waist and kissed her tenderly on the cheek. "I wasn't sure if I should come or not—you never called me back."

Denise stared in disappointment at the blue jeans and striped rugby shirt Winston was wearing. "Winnie—why didn't you dress up? It's a semiformal party."

"How was I supposed to know?" Winston shrugged. "You haven't been returning my calls."

With Bruce waiting for her in the kitchen, it was not a good time to start a fight with Winston. Denise felt like she was suddenly being pulled in a thousand directions at once. "I've been busy, Winston. I have a huge biology midterm on Wednesday and I have to take care of things for my aunt. I have a lot on my mind."

"It only takes two seconds to pick up the phone," Winston said.

Denise's face grew hot. "I don't have time for this now, Winston."

"Don't get mad," he said, looking hurt. "I'll go home and change if that's what you want."

Perfect, then I'll have a little more time to talk to Bruce. Denise nodded. "Maybe you should."

Denise left Winston and went back to the kitchen. Thankfully, Bruce was still waiting for her. He'd shed his expensive suit jacket, rolled the sleeves of his dress shirt up to the elbows, and loosened his silk tie. "I was wondering if you were going to come back," he said.

Denise rolled her eyes. "I don't know how much more of this I can take, Bruce. It's hard to keep a secret from Winston. I feel like I'm leading a double life."

"Maybe we should follow through on your plan soon," he suggested, snagging a jumbo shrimp from a platter and dunking it in cocktail sauce. "Before the end of the week."

"Not until after my bio exam on Wednesday," Denise said. "I need all my concentration. When's Lila coming back?"

"The middle of next week. We have plenty of time."

Denise sighed with relief. She reached distractedly for the seafood platter behind Bruce and dipped a shrimp in the sauce. As she brought the morsel toward her, Bruce turned around quickly, and a great big blob of cocktail sauce landed on his tie.

"Oh no!" Denise groaned in embarrassment. "Look at your tie—I'm so sorry." She grabbed a clean dish towel and dampened it under the faucet. "Let me clean it up for you."

"Please, Denise," Bruce insisted. "It's all right. I have a thousand other ties like this one."

"I'm such a klutz!" Denise held the top of

12

the tie flat against Bruce's strong chest and worked on the darkened spot near the bottom of the tie. The more she rubbed the spot, the worse the stain became.

"Really, Denise—it's no problem. . . ."

Denise tossed the towel on the counter. She was determined to get the spot out. "Maybe if you take the tie off, I could run it under some cold water." She undid the knot and slipped the tie off his neck.

Bruce undid the top two buttons of his shirt. "That's a lot better," he said.

"Denise?"

Denise whirled around, startled, the tie still in her hands. "Winston, you scared the living daylights out of me."

"Sorry," he said slowly, looking down at the tie. "I—uh—I just wanted to ask you what you wanted me to change into."

Now that Denise and Bruce's plan was set in motion, she suddenly felt herself growing more calm. "Just wear what you've got on, Winnie," she said. "It doesn't matter."

At breakfast Tuesday morning Winston numbly carried his tray to a quiet table in the corner of the cafeteria and stared down at the cold scrambled eggs on his plate. They looked as pathetic as he felt. He'd spent the entire night wide awake in bed, unable to get rid of the memory of seeing Denise and Bruce cozying up to each other in the kitchen. *Denise is going to leave me for Bruce.* The words pounded in his head like a jackhammer.

"I hear that if you stare at cafeteria eggs long enough, you can actually see them move," someone said.

For a brief second Winston hoped it was Denise, but he knew better than to expect her to show up for breakfast after what happened last night. Instead the voice belonged to Denise's sorority sister, Jessica Wakefield. "Hi, Jess," Winston said without looking up.

"Mind if I sit here? Or are you expecting Denise?"

Winston raised his heavy head and looked up at Jessica, who was decked out in a black leather skirt and red cropped sweater. "It looks like Denise stood me up," he said sourly. "Have a seat."

Jessica ripped open four packets of sugar and dumped them into her coffee. "Where are your glasses? Did you get contacts?" Jessica asked, sipping her coffee.

Winston nodded. "A few days ago."

"I like them," Jessica said, grinning with approval. "They make you look more sophisticated."

"Thanks," Winston answered shyly. He took a bite of scrambled eggs, but for some reason he couldn't seem to swallow them.

They rolled around in his mouth as he searched for something to say to Jessica. He wasn't in the mood for making small talk.

"Does Denise like them?"

Winston poked at his breakfast. "She hasn't had much time to really notice. She's been busy."

"You two were together at the party last night. She must've noticed them then, right?" Jessica asked.

Bruce's deep laughter bellowed through the cafeteria. Winston stared glassily across the room to the Sigma table, where the enemy sat. Bruce was at the middle of the table, looking enormously muscular in his leather Sigma jacket. He was telling a story, using his brilliant smile and engaging presence to captivate every single person within a four-foot radius. Winston's heart sank. Bruce had looks, charm, status—even a slick black Porsche that Winston would die to drive. He had everything that Winston could only dream of. It wasn't a shock that Denise would be attracted to Bruce. The sad part of it was, Winston understood completely.

"What do you think of Bruce Patman?" Winston suddenly blurted.

Tapping a long, manicured fingernail against the side of the coffee cup, Jessica stared at him blankly. "I think he's a total jerk—a victim of a tragic love affair with himself. Plus he has an ego the size of Texas. Why do you ask?"

"No reason," Winston said, shaking his head.

Jessica delicately put down her coffee cup. "It's Denise, isn't it?" she asked gently.

Winston looked up. "How did you know?"

"I don't want to alarm you, but I saw something at the party last night that you should know about," Jessica said in a confidential whisper. She sent a chilly look in Bruce's direction. "Lila's in Paris, Winston. As the saying goes, while the cat's away, the mouse will play."

Chapter Two

"How are those letters coming, Winston?" Dean Franklin walked through the doorway of Winston's tiny side office, checking the expensive gold watch on his wrist. "The mail room closes at four, and I want to make sure we get them out."

"I have a few more envelopes to address and then I'll be done." Winston looked at the impossibly large pile of envelopes he'd somehow managed to assemble in one short afternoon. For the moment work was the only thing that could keep his mind off Denise and Bruce. Winston stuffed envelopes at lightning speed as if it were the only way to outrun the wild thoughts charging through his mind like a herd of buffalo.

The dean gave Winston a fatherly nod and placed a firm hand on his shoulder. "I just

17

want you to know, Winston, how pleased I am with the wonderful work you've been doing. I really appreciate it."

"Thanks, sir," Winston answered with a modest smile. "I plan on staying here for a long time."

"That's what I like to hear." Dean Franklin's intelligent blue eyes glimmered with approval. He walked over to the antique oak coatrack and removed his overcoat and hat from one of the fancy carved knobs. "I'm leaving early today. Amanda and I are having a cocktail party this evening and I have to get ready for it. If you don't have any other plans, we'd be pleased to have you."

Winston's dark eyebrows arched a fraction of an inch. "A party?"

"It's for the university trustees," Dean Franklin explained. "Once a year we have a little get-together at my house. I thought it might give you a chance to meet some of the people you'll be dealing with on the phone. I'd really like for you to be there if you can make it."

Schmoozing with the rich and powerful wasn't something Winston was accustomed to—but he couldn't refuse an invite from his new boss. "It sounds great," he said with enthusiasm. "I'll be there."

Dean Franklin buttoned his gray overcoat and put on his fedora. "The party's a little on the dressy side—do you have a suit?"

"Sure," Winston answered casually. In the back of his mind he recalled a simple navy blue suit he'd worn to his high school graduation and probably should've worn to the Theta party last night. At the moment it was hanging in the back of his closet, probably dusty and in urgent need of cleaning. Winston crossed his fingers, hoping the suit still fit.

Picking up his black leather briefcase, the dean eyed the picture of Denise on Winston's desk. "Your girlfriend is welcome to come too. I'd love to meet her."

Denise would love to go to a party like this. If Denise's interest was shifting to a social climber like Bruce Patman, then she'd definitely be impressed to hear that Winston had gotten himself invited to one of the university's most important social events of the year. The party could be the very thing that saved their relationship. *Bruce isn't the only one with connections,* he thought proudly.

"I'm sure she'd be happy to come," Winston said brightly.

"Wonderful." Dean Franklin headed toward the door. "I'll see you around seven."

With an explosive burst of energy, Winston resumed his work of stuffing and addressing envelopes. He worked at a rapid pace, whistling happily to himself, anxious to finish

19

the mail so that he could track down Denise and give her the good news. He couldn't wait to see the look of surprise. She'd be so happy and impressed with Winston that she'd never even glance in Bruce's direction again.

"Sorry, Winnie," Denise said casually as she pulled an oversize green plaid shirt out of her closet and tied it around her waist. "I already have plans for the evening."

Winston blinked at her uncomprehendingly, as though she'd just spoken to him in some exotic dialect. "What do you mean?" he pouted, throwing himself onto the powder blue futon in the middle of Denise's dorm room.

"I mean I can't go to the party," Denise answered, eyeing him strangely. Winston had been acting weird lately, as though there was something heavy on his mind, but he just didn't have the courage to spit it out.

The heels of Winston's sneakered feet tapped rhythmically on the striped Guatemalan throw rug that covered half of Denise's floor. "I thought you'd be impressed," he mumbled like a scolded child. "I thought you'd be dying to go."

Denise exhaled, her shoulders sagging tiredly. She had too much to get done in the next few hours to be able to deal with one of Winston's crises. "Winnie, my wanting to go has nothing to do with it," she said as delicately as possible, turning away from his brooding expression. Opening her canvas tote bag, she loaded it up with textbooks, a notebook, and a handful of pens. "I have a huge bio exam tomorrow that I have to study for. I'm going to go to the beach house where it's quiet so I can get a lot of work done."

"We don't have to stay long," he persisted. "The dean is expecting you."

Denise shook her curly head. What was it going to take to make him understand? "This test is worth almost as much as the final. I can't blow it off," she said tiredly. "Tell the dean I'm sorry I couldn't make it. I'm sure he'll be more understanding than you are at the moment."

"I went to your sorority party," Winston argued with a pleading, puppy-dog look in his brown eyes. His pounding feet quickened their rhythm.

A sudden surge of intense irritation made Denise drop the bag with an angry thud. She stared at him, folding her arms across her chest. "The Theta party was different. I told you about it weeks in advance. You, on the other hand, just breeze in here two hours before a formal cocktail party and expect that I'll automatically stop whatever I'm doing and follow you."

Winston leaned his head back and glared at the white paper lantern covering the ceiling light. "Thanks for taking such an interest in my life," he answered bitterly.

"Thanks for being so mature about this," Denise shot back. As soon as her mouth formed the words, she instantly wished she could take them back. The harshness of her own voice made her flinch. *I don't want it to be like this,* she told herself.

Sinking to the floor, Denise reached out and encircled Winston's neck with her tan, slender arms. "I'm sorry, Winnie," she whispered in his ear. Her lips traced a path up toward his temple, which she covered with a sweet kiss. "I didn't mean it. I'm thrilled that you were invited to the party. It's an important event."

Winston turned toward her, biting his lip to suppress a smile. "Does that mean you'll go with me?" he asked.

Leaning against him, Denise pressed her forehead to his and closed her eyes. "I'm sorry, but the answer's still no. I hope you understand."

"Oh, I understand," Winston answered, pulling away from her. "I understand perfectly."

"Hi, honey, I'm home!" Jessica shouted as she burst through the door of her dorm room with a large vegetarian pizza and a two-liter bottle of soda. She smiled brightly. "I've brought you dinner and gossip!"

Elizabeth Wakefield, who was standing in front of her open closet in a satin slip, turned away from her wardrobe and greeted her twin sister with an identical smile. It was nice to see that Jessica had taken the initiative to pick up dinner for once—just like everything else, she usually left the responsibility up to Elizabeth.

"Dinner first," Elizabeth said, her blue-green eyes fixed on the pizza. Her stomach rumbled in agreement. "I'm absolutely starving."

Setting the pizza box down on their makeshift cinder block coffee table, Jessica gave her twin a quick once-over. "Dressing up a little for sister night, aren't we?"

"Sorry, Jess, but I'm going to have to bail on our plans," Elizabeth answered before sinking her teeth into a gooey slice.

Jessica frowned, draping her long legs over the arm of the love seat as she fell back onto the cushions. "What's the excuse this time? Are you working at the station tonight, slaving away on some journalistic masterpiece?"

Elizabeth shook her head. Grabbing two clean mugs from off the bookshelf, she filled them with soda and handed one to her sister. "It's a party."

Jessica bolted upright, nearly spilling the soda all over the floor. "Did you say *party*? How come *I* wasn't invited?"

"Because it's for the university trustees, that's why," Elizabeth answered. "Dean Franklin is having a cocktail party at his house."

23

Jessica rolled her eyes. "I'm sorry, Liz, but a bunch of stuffed shirts and a few cocktails does not a party make. You need cool tunes, hot guys—"

"And warm beer?" Elizabeth interjected.

"Not even," Jessica answered with authority. "Just the hot guys will do."

Elizabeth took another bite of pizza and returned to her open closet in search of something to wear. Unlike her gregarious twin, Elizabeth much preferred a quiet evening at home to a party any day. "Well, whatever you call this little gathering, the fact is, I have to be there. Tom was supposed to do a story on it, but he's got a deadline to meet. I told him I'd go in his place."

Sighing loudly, Jessica reached for a slice. "The ever dutiful girlfriend."

"It was the least I could do," Elizabeth said, going through her neatly organized closet. "I'm going to meet up with him at the station later tonight to help out."

"Who's going to watch old movies with me?" Jessica puckered her lips into a soft pout.

"We'll do it another night. I promise." Elizabeth pulled a conservative brown linen skirt and jacket set off a hanger and held them against her body. "What do you think?"

Jessica gave the suit an unenthusiastic thumbs-down. "Too drab." She pointed to her own messy pile of dirty clothes that covered her bed.

"You can borrow my leopard print cat suit or the micromini I just bought. If I were you, I'd even go with what you're wearing right now."

Looking down at the flimsy slip she was wearing, Elizabeth smirked. "I'm sure you would," she answered dryly. "Thanks for the fashion tip, Jess, but I think I'll stick with the suit."

Elizabeth zipped the back of the skirt and buttoned a cream-colored silky shirt with a reluctant sigh. She wasn't in the mood to interview campus bigwigs about the university's budget; all she wanted to do was to stay home, crawl into her favorite pajamas, and watch some classic movies with her sister.

Jessica swung her legs around and sat up with a sudden urgency. "So, do you want to hear the gossip?"

Elizabeth nodded furiously. She was anxious to stop feeling sorry for herself. "What happened?"

"Well—guess who I had breakfast with this morning," Jessica said coyly. A slow, secretive smile crossed her face. "Winston Egbert."

Elizabeth slipped on a pair of very businesslike brown leather pumps. "So what's the big news about Winston?"

Jessica kicked off her flip-flops and propped her bare feet on the coffee table, perilously close to the pizza. "It seems he's having a little trouble with Denise," she said dramatically, savoring every juicy word. "He thinks she's cheating on him."

"No way!" Elizabeth's eyes widened with shock. Ever since she'd known Winston and Denise, they seemed like a great couple. "With whom?"

"Bruce Patman."

Elizabeth laughed so hard, it took a moment for her to catch her breath. "That is the most absurd thing I've ever heard. I can't imagine Denise going for someone like Bruce. Besides, he's seeing Lila."

"She's out of the country for the week," Jessica said heavily.

"So?"

"And Denise has been avoiding Winston lately, being really secretive," Jessica added. "At the Theta party last night Winston caught them together in the kitchen."

"There's no crime in talking to someone else," Elizabeth answered rationally, buttoning up her suit jacket.

"She was undoing his tie, Liz."

Elizabeth paused for a moment. It *was* pretty damaging evidence. "It's all circumstantial—I'm sure there's a good explanation for it."

Jessica examined her long pink fingernails. "Anyhow, Winston seemed pretty down about it. I tried my best to cheer him up."

"What did you say?" Elizabeth asked.

"I told him that I thought he was right

26

because before he showed up at the party, I saw Denise leading Bruce by the hand into the kitchen," Jessica answered.

Elizabeth covered her face with her hands and shook her head. "Jess—you didn't!"

"What's wrong with saying that?" Jessica asked. "He needs to know the truth."

Elizabeth pinned her long blond hair into a loose chignon. "I'm sure you only made the poor guy feel worse." Winston had been a good friend of hers since high school, and Elizabeth knew that it didn't take much to make him feel insecure. "I bet the whole thing is just some sort of weird misunderstanding. Denise wouldn't leave Winston for Bruce."

One of Jessica's eyebrows arched skeptically. "Who knows, Liz. Stranger things have happened."

"You look hot tonight, Winston—if I do say so myself," Winston said to his reflection as he stood before the full-length mirror on the back of his door. "Denise's going to be sorry she didn't go with you to the dean's party." Thankfully, the suit he'd worn in high school still fit. Sure, the suit jacket was a little snug—but everything was fine as long as he kept his arms at his sides. There was absolutely nothing wrong with his white shirt, and the blue-and-purple-striped clip-on tie he wore virtually guaranteed the perfect knot. But it was his new contacts that really made the difference. It instantly transformed Winston from college kid into a man.

"Hi—my name is Winston Egbert . . . I'm Dean Franklin's assistant." Winston practiced introducing himself to an imaginary trustee, adjusting the depth of his voice and the firmness of his handshake in search of the perfect greeting. But his confidence wavered every time he thought of all the important people who were going to be there. *You can do it,* said a little voice inside his head. *You don't need Denise to socialize; you'll do just fine by yourself.*

Winston dabbed his hair with gel and combed it through. Any thought of Denise made the muscles in his chest seize up. He was beginning to have serious doubts about her going to the beach house to study. If it had been a horse race, Winston would've bet his life savings that Denise had a date with Bruce instead. But he desperately wanted to believe he was wrong.

At ten minutes to eight Winston grabbed his room keys and headed toward Dickenson Hall to pick up Elizabeth—they were going to walk to the party together. The dean and his wife lived in an elegant, three-story colonial house on the edge of campus. Many times Winston had passed by the property, admiring the four white pillars and the brick circular driveway. He'd always wondered what the place looked like on the inside, and now he was finally about to find out.

"Hey there, Winston," Elizabeth said, meeting him near the entrance to her dorm. "Are you ready for the big party?"

"I'm always ready for stuffy conversation," Winston joked, even though his insides were nervously churning. They walked down the path toward the road. "How about you?"

Elizabeth held up her notepad filled with interview questions for the trustees. "It's going to be a blast." Her smile faded into a serious expression. "You know, Winston, I talked to Jessica—is everything going OK with you?"

Winston stuck his hands into the pockets of his suit jacket. "She told you, huh?"

Elizabeth nodded. "I wasn't there at the party, but I have to say that appearances can be deceiving sometimes. It may not have been what you think."

"I don't know what I think anymore, Liz." Winston watched the warm orange rays of the setting sun spread their shimmering light over the deep green contours of the campus lawn. "Denise doesn't seem to be the person I thought she was, our relationship isn't what I thought it was—but maybe I'm wrong. I'd *love* to be wrong."

Elizabeth was quiet. Winston squinted into the bright light as he looked across the quad. Several yards ahead he saw a familiar figure dressed in ripped jeans and a green plaid shirt, sitting on the library steps. Denise. Even from a distance he could see the way each of her brown curls captured the light perfectly. Winston's heart seemed to stop before it resumed its natural rhythm at twice the normal speed.

Winston halted. Elizabeth looked at him strangely. "What's wrong. . . ." Her words trailed off as she followed his gaze to the library steps.

Winston shielded his eyes with his hand, cutting the glare from the setting sun. *She's talking to someone*, he decided. Squinting slightly, Winston was trying to figure out whom Denise was talking to, when suddenly the person stood up. The dark hair and muscular build were dead giveaways. It was Bruce Patman.

Elizabeth gently touched Winston's elbow. "They're just talking, Winston. They're not doing anything wrong."

"She lied to me," Winston said through gritted teeth. "She said she was going to the beach house to study. She should've left an hour ago."

Denise threw back her head and laughed. Bruce laughed too, clutching his sides. They seemed to be having a great time. Neither one of them noticed Elizabeth or Winston. *Are they laughing at me?* Winston wondered. Every time he saw them together, it felt as if he'd just swallowed a metal burr that rolled around, painfully tearing at his insides.

"I guess I wasn't being paranoid at all—the evidence is right in front of me." Winston's eyes blurred as he fought back hot tears. His worst suspicions were confirmed. Denise and Bruce *were* seeing each other behind his back.

"Why don't you go up and talk to them?" Elizabeth suggested. "I bet there's a good explanation."

"There's no point—it's too late." Ever since Denise became Winston's girlfriend, he had known deep in his heart that he would eventually lose her to someone else. Someone better. Denise was so outgoing and smart and so beautiful that Winston was just grateful for every day they shared together. He'd known that it was just a matter of time before Denise looked elsewhere.

And that time is now, Winston thought sadly, dropping his hands limply at his sides. A hollow emptiness invaded his body, eroding the blissful happiness Denise had brought him while they were together. Winston had a sudden and complete understanding of the rage others in his position might experience, but he himself didn't feel it. It would have been easy to walk right up to both Denise and Bruce and lash out at them. Instead Winston turned on his heels and headed down a different path, a quiet feeling of defeat settling in the middle of his torso.

"Come on, Elizabeth," Winston said, looking around. "Let's get out of here."

Chapter
Three

"What would you like to see the university do to improve this year's budget?" Elizabeth asked for what seemed like the hundredth time. She had been systematically working her way through the gathering of trustees, starting from the elegant and spacious living room of the dean's house, out the French doors, and beyond, to the stone patio. *As soon as I make it to the far side of the pool I'm out of here,* Elizabeth promised herself, anxious to get back to the station to help Tom. She had planned to leave over an hour ago, but the trustees' long-winded answers eliminated that prospect.

"I'm glad you asked me that, miss," boomed Arthur Rubble IV, heir to the Rubble bubble gum fortune and benefactor to Sweet Valley University. Arthur was round, soft, and pink, much like the gooey substance that had made his great-grandfather so famous. "I believe the curse of today's universities is waste." His puffy lips stretched and contracted around a huge wad of gum. "Let me tell you something—Arthur Rubble the First didn't make his fortune by wasting money."

I've got a real live one here, Elizabeth mused, stifling a yawn. She had interviewed enough bigwigs in the past to know that Arthur Rubble had no trouble filling his bubbles with hot air. "What suggestions do you have for cutting waste?" Elizabeth grabbed a champagne glass filled with seltzer and a slice of lemon from a nearby waiter and settled in for the long haul.

"The first thing you do is cut back on the little things and work your way up," Rubble whispered confidentially. His fleshy jowls jiggled as he spoke. "It forces people to conserve and makes them more creative. With a bit of ingenuity, we can all get by on a lot less."

Where did Winston run off to? It'd be nice to talk to someone I know for a change, Elizabeth thought, sighing inwardly as her eyes scanned the patio crowd. Nearly everyone at the party had a good twenty years on her and she was beginning to feel painfully out of place. "What specifically did you have in mind?" she asked, sipping her seltzer.

"The best thing to do is replace expensive products with cheaper materials." Arthur folded his arms across his broad paunch. "Take Rubble Bubble, for example. It's inexpensive and fun, and did you know it has over a thousand and one household uses?"

"I wasn't aware of that." Elizabeth suddenly felt very tired. If Arthur had any intention of running down the entire list of uses for his chewing gum, it was conceivable that she'd be there all night. "But how exactly does this affect the university?"

"SVU could replace many of their expensive office supplies with Rubble Bubble to save money." Arthur popped the glossy wad of gum out of his mouth and squished it between his fingers. "It can be used as a paper adhesive, replacing both staples and tape. Leave the gum out to dry overnight and it makes a great eraser!"

Elizabeth covered her mouth demurely, holding back laughter. Was this guy for real? While Arthur extolled the virtues of his gum, Elizabeth stole discreet glances past him, looking for any means of escape.

"In the first year alone we could cut the office supply budget in half!" Arthur continued on. "Imagine the money we could save if we used Rubble Bubble to patch holes in dorm walls and leaks in plumbing!"

There's Winston. He can help me get out of here. Elizabeth caught a glimpse of him at the far end of the patio. He was sitting by himself on a fancy wrought-iron garden bench at the other end of the pool.

Arthur's tiny pink-rimmed eyes held a dreamy expression as he stared up at the starry sky. "My ultimate dream is to see pieces of Rubble Bubble laid end to end as floor tiling in every building on campus."

"I hope I live to see your dream come true," Elizabeth said evenly, stretching out her hand. "Thank you for your time, Mr. Rubble. It was a pleasure talking to you."

"The pleasure was all mine," Arthur said, slipping a pack of Rubble Bubble to her as they shook hands. "Try using it to tack up your posters—it works wonders."

Elizabeth gave him a quick but polite smile and headed toward the end of the patio where Winston had been sitting. *I hope he's doing all right,* she thought, remembering the walk over. It *had* looked pretty suspicious the way Denise and Bruce were laughing together, but again, Elizabeth was certain that the explanation was a good one. Denise and Winston had been so great together, it was unthinkable that she'd leave him for someone else.

Elizabeth was just about to walk up and take the empty seat next to Winston when suddenly Amanda Franklin, the dean's wife, slid right next to him. She was wearing a low-cut, aqua-colored evening gown with silver sequin trim and a high slit that showed off her long legs. Amanda snuggled up very close to Winston, running her fingers up and down his arm.

That's strange, Elizabeth thought. *It looks like she's flirting with him.* She stopped in her tracks and took refuge behind a large potted tree so that Winston wouldn't see her. He certainly didn't look like a guy who'd just caught his girl-friend with someone else. In fact, he looked as though he was having a pretty good time.

Peering through the leaves, Elizabeth shook her head sadly. Denise and Winston couldn't have been separated for more than a day or two, and already he was flirting with another woman—and not just any woman, but the dean's wife. Elizabeth turned around and headed back inside the house. She couldn't stand to watch another moment.

"Be careful, Winston," Elizabeth whispered into the evening breeze, "or you might get in way over your head."

"Have another glass of champagne," Amanda Franklin coaxed, her fingers tracing playful paths around Winston's collar. Dean Franklin was standing only a few feet away, on the other side of the rose trellis, talking with a small circle of tuxedoed trustees. Everyone seemed deeply submerged in the topics of bud-get cuts, government subsidies, and financial forecasts—everyone, that is, except Winston and Amanda.

Winston had had enough to drink, but it seemed impossible to say the word *no* whenever Amanda was around. "I—I suppose one more glass wouldn't hurt," Winston said with a smile as he took the glass from her. The airy feeling in his head overshadowed the heaviness of his heart. With the tranquil blue-green light of the pool dancing across Amanda's skin, Denise seemed a million miles away.

You had your chance, Denise, Winston thought, sipping his champagne. *And you blew it.*

Amanda traced the rim of her glass with her fingertip. "It's good, isn't it?" she said before knocking back nearly half the glass in one graceful motion. Amanda kept crossing and re-crossing her long, smooth legs, rubbing her calf against his every time she moved.

"Hmmm . . . ," Winston hummed contentedly, waiting for her to cross her legs again. "It's a gorgeous night," he said, running his fingers through his thick brown hair. The evening breeze was refreshing against his hot face and neck. Winston gazed up at the cool moon, a wafer-thin disk he imagined melting like a peppermint on his tongue. On a night like this, anything was possible.

"It *is* gorgeous," Amanda cooed, her lips lurking dangerously close to his ear. She kicked off her silver sandals, revealing an exquisitely shaped foot, then ran her sexy red toenails up and down his leg. "What do you say we take a walk out back? I'd love to show you the garden in the moonlight."

I wish I'd gotten my contacts sooner, Winston thought to himself. He had no idea that with them he'd become irresistible to women, especially to someone as gorgeous as Amanda. Warm rivers ran under Winston's skin, carrying him away without reason or fear of consequence. He didn't want to think; he only wanted to act impulsively, letting his instincts guide the journey.

Winston turned his head toward her so that their lips were almost touching. "W-What's in the garden?" he asked in a husky voice.

"Many surprises," Amanda whispered, her mouth so close to his that Winston could breathe in her words. She slid her hand underneath the lapel of his sport coat and pressed her hand against his chest. "I can make you forget the terrible things Denise has done to you."

"Oh, really?" Winston said with a flirtatious laugh. "How do you plan on doing that?"

Amanda brushed the hair out of Winston's eyes. "You're just going to have to find out for yourself," she said coyly. "But I guarantee a night you'll never forget."

Winston's desire was so strong that every muscle ached to be with Amanda. Her soft, full lips, her dark eyes, the way she moved her beautiful body—everything about her drew him in like a vortex. The longing was too great. He didn't want to wait to go to the garden to be with her. Winston closed his eyes, dying to feel the heat of her kiss.

Just as the feathery touch of Amanda's lips brushed his, she pushed him away. "It would be too suspicious if we walked out to the garden together. I'll leave first and you can meet me out back in a few minutes," she whispered. Her breath sent a sizzling shiver down Winston's back. "I can't wait to show you around."

Winston nodded numbly, watching as Amanda walked away. The way her long, golden curls fell softly down to the middle of her back, how the sleek, gauzy layers of her aqua dress clung to her curves made Winston breathless. Amanda turned slightly, looking over her shoulder and giving him a coy wink. She was a mythical mermaid in a sea of crusty old penguins.

A few moments later, just as Winston was about to follow his urges out to the garden, Dean Franklin appeared out of nowhere, patting him on the back. "I hope you're taking good care of my wife."

Winston stiffened. Had he seen anything? "Sorry, sir?"

"I appreciate you keeping her company,"

the dean said. "She never finds anyone she enjoys talking to at these things."

Smiling weakly, Winston struggled to maintain the evening's magic, but it was rapidly dissolving. "Amanda's an intriguing woman," he answered.

Dean Franklin looked around. "I don't see your girlfriend anywhere—is she here?"

Winston shook his head, which was becoming heavier every second. The memories he'd been trying to avoid all evening came flooding back to him like a high tide. "Denise had a test to study for—but she sends her regards."

Dean Franklin nodded with approval. "Academics must come first, of course. Please tell her I look forward to meeting her at some other time."

"I will."

Dean Franklin flashed Winston a gracious, trusting smile. "I'll see you at work tomorrow?"

Winston tried to swallow the hard, bitter lump that had formed in his throat. "Of course—nine o'clock sharp."

With a gentle nod the dean moved on to greet the rest of his guests.

What on earth am I doing? Winston questioned himself, trying not to think about Amanda's warm body waiting for him out back in the silvery, moonlit garden. *A night you'll never forget.* Winston took a deep breath, hoping the fresh air would sober him up a little and curb the overpowering passion inside him. *She's the dean's wife*, Winston reminded himself. *Even if she is incredibly gorgeous, she's still the dean's wife.*

"I have to get out of here," Winston muttered under his breath. Seeing the dean was like a splash of icy cold water, plunging him back to reality. Winston shuddered—it had been an incredibly close call, but somehow he'd managed to avoid disaster. But if he ran into Amanda again, Winston wasn't so sure he'd be able to trust himself.

Quickly Winston walked through the French doors and hurried through the house. He thought of Amanda waiting alone in the garden. Would she be hurt, or would she understand that betraying his boss was something he just couldn't bring himself to do?

Just as Winston reached for the doorknob, he heard a voice calling to him from the kitchen. "You're not going to leave without saying good-bye, are you?"

Winston whipped around. Amanda was leaning seductively against the kitchen counter, a fresh glass of champagne in her hand. A few guests lingered, their eyebrows raised curiously.

"Thank you for a wonderful evening," Winston said, formally holding out his hand for her to shake. "You have a lovely home."

The corners of Amanda's mouth turned up

42

in a wry smile. She took his hand and yanked him toward her. "Where were you? I waited for you," she whispered in his ear.

"I—I know," Winston stammered. "I'm sorry. I couldn't. I *wanted* to, but . . ." His voice trailed off.

Amanda turned his hand over and traced the lines of his palm with the tips of her fingers. "You have very clear lines."

"Are you a palm reader?" Winston asked lightly, feeling a thin film of sweat form on his forehead.

"Oh yes," Amanda breathed. "It says right here that you will find happiness with an older woman."

Winston laughed nervously, looking around to see if anyone was watching. Everyone had gone out to the patio. Before Winston could pull back his hand, Amanda had raised it to her lips and was kissing his palm, working her way to his wrist and arm.

"Please—stop it!" Winston pulled away, battling against the desire that was resurging. He tried to ignore the electric tingle that was working its way down his spine. "Look— Amanda—I have to go."

"I plan on seeing more of you, Winston," Amanda said, her brown eyes traveling the length of his body. "A lot more."

*   *   *

Elizabeth was almost at the end of the Franklins' driveway when she heard the front door slam. She turned around to see Winston, red-faced and panting, scurrying down the steps.

"Are you going back to your dorm?" he called, jogging over to where she was.

Elizabeth stopped and waited. He didn't look well—his eyes were glassy and he had a skittish, almost paranoid way about him. "I'm going to the WSVU station."

"I'll walk you over there," he said decidedly.

"Winston, are you all right?" she asked as they walked toward the road together. "You seem kind of nervous."

"I'm fine," he said quickly. "Did you have fun at the party?"

Elizabeth clutched her notebook, full of notes on her conversations with the trustees. "No—it was pretty boring," she answered. "How about you?"

There was a long pause. Elizabeth looked at Winston, who was staring at the ground as he walked. He seemed to be too deep in thought to have heard her. *Maybe he's thinking about Denise,* Elizabeth decided. But there had to be more to it than that. He'd seemed to be having a great time at the party, especially whenever Amanda was in the vicinity. *Did something happen between them?*

"Winston?"

44

He looked up at her, startled. "Huh?"

"If you need to talk about something, I'm here, you know," Elizabeth said.

Winston wiped his sweaty brow with his jacket sleeve. "What do you mean?" he asked testily.

Elizabeth was taken aback. "I'm a friend. If something's bothering you, you can tell me. That's all."

He looked at her strangely, as if she were an international spy who'd just asked him to hand over top secret documents. "Nothing's bothering me, Liz."

You could've fooled me, she thought. "OK— I'm sorry I said anything. I was only trying to help."

If Winston had been acting like his normal self, at this point in the conversation he would have apologized. *Or at least said something,* Elizabeth thought. But he just walked on, looking at the ground, letting the silence fall between them like a lead curtain. Elizabeth made no further attempt to get Winston to open up for the entire walk back to campus.

"This is my stop," Elizabeth said lightly when they reached the WSVU building. "I'll see you tomorrow."

Still deeply entrenched in his own world, Winston walked on without saying another word.

*   *   *

After walking Elizabeth to the campus TV station, Winston headed back to Oakley Hall to turn in for the night. The foggy haze of alcohol still lingered, but it had dissipated just enough to remind him of the pain he'd spent all evening trying to bury deep inside himself. *Denise doesn't want to be with me anymore,* Winston thought sullenly, dragging his feet up the stairs to the third floor. The remnants of champagne, combined with the memory of Denise on the library steps with Bruce, was a potent cocktail that sent Winston's head reeling, making him feel even more empty and vulnerable than before.

"Welcome back to your empty room, Winston," he said aloud to himself as he opened the door. He walked into the dark room, not even bothering to turn on the lights. Winston was too ashamed to face himself, especially after the way he had acted at the dean's house. But he wasn't entirely to blame—Amanda had done most of the flirting. The problem was that he wasn't very good at stopping her. Amanda was one of the sexiest, most beautiful women he had ever seen.

But at least I managed to get out of there before things got way out of hand, Winston told himself, pulling up the window blinds. But it was little comfort. The room was flooded with silver moonbeams, the cold light casting an odd, surreal glow on the window frame, the desk, and the end of Winston's bed. The rest of the room retreated into black shadows. Leaning against the sill, Winston peered down at the dark, empty pathway below and the neatly trimmed hedge that wrapped around the corner of the building. He found himself longing to see the garden Amanda had been speaking of, to discover the surprises that awaited him there.

Stop thinking about her. Winston took off his suit jacket and draped it across the back of his desk chair, a sudden chill gripping him. Had anyone seen them flirting tonight at the party? Amanda was hardly discreet. If the dean found out, it would definitely mean the end of Winston's dream job, if not his entire college career. It was stupid to take such a risk, even if Amanda *was* completely irresistible. Winston sat on the edge of the bed and took out his contacts, carefully putting them away in their case. *From now on,* he resolved silently, *I'm going to stay as far away from Amanda Franklin as possible.* Spending any time alone with her would only spell disaster.

Just as Winston started unbuttoning the cuffs of his dress shirt, he heard a gentle knock on the door.

"Who is it?" he asked.

There was no answer—only another knock,

slightly more urgent this time. *Maybe it's Denise,* he silently hoped. *Maybe she's decided to come back to me.*

"Coming!" Winston ran to the door and yanked it open. Through the fuzzy blur of his nearsighted eyes Winston caught the outline of a female figure dressed in a trench coat, holding a coffee cup in each hand.

"Did I catch you at a bad time?" the woman asked. As she stepped toward him Amanda's gorgeous features came into focus.

Before Winston had a chance to answer, Amanda was already pushing him backward into his room, her stiletto heels tapping decisively across the floor. Winston's heart slammed against his rib cage. "What are you doing here?" he asked, swiftly turning on the overhead light.

Amanda reached up and turned the light off again. "The party got so boring after you left," she said in a throaty voice, thrusting one of the paper cups in his face. "Cappuccino?"

"No, thanks—I've given up caffeine." Winston nervously shifted his weight from one foot to the other. He swallowed hard. *I can't let her stay,* he told himself.

Amanda pouted flirtatiously as she set the two cups down on Winston's bureau. The coat she was wearing was much too big for her; it was wrapped tightly around her body and tied securely with the belt. Squinting, Winston realized that the coat she was wearing belonged to the dean.

"You're not being a very good host, Winston."

"S-Sorry," Winston gushed, although he wasn't exactly sure why he had to apologize. His cheeks were flushed. "Would you like to sit down?"

"Not really—but I'd like to put my coat somewhere," she said, loosening the belt.

Winston held his arm out to take the coat, but Amanda let it slip off her shoulders and cascade to the floor. His jaw dropped when he saw what she was wearing underneath—a sexy red silk chemise.

Amanda stepped away from the coat, leaving it in a crumpled heap on the floor, and moved closer to Winston. "You're awfully quiet," she said, playing with his necktie. "Don't you have anything to say for yourself?"

Winston opened his mouth to answer, but something seemed to short-circuit in his brain, preventing him from forming an intelligible sentence. When he didn't answer, Amanda yanked on his tie to pull him closer, but the metal clip released, leaving the necktie in her hands and Winston standing frozen in place. A wry laugh escaped from her long, slender throat as she tossed the tie over her shoulder. "Shall I try again?"

A froglike squeak was the only sound Winston could manage. His heart went into overdrive and blood raced through his veins at lightning speed. *Should I do this?* Winston struggled with the pros and cons of the situation, but his reasoning became muddy and clouded as his instincts kicked into high gear.

This time Amanda didn't wait for a response. Grabbing his collar firmly in both hands, she pulled Winston against her and tried to kiss him deeply. Winston's lips were tightly locked, his body passive and lifeless.

Frustrated by his seeming lack of interest, Amanda pulled away. "What's wrong with you?"

"N-Nothing," Winston answered languidly, his knees weakening. "I just—I don't think that this is a very good idea." He turned on the overhead light again.

Amanda's brown eyes turned liquid, almost sad. "You don't find me attractive?"

"Of course I do." Winston covered his face with his hands. How did this suddenly become so complicated?

"No one can see us; no one will know," she whispered, turning off the light. In the darkness the moonglow illuminated Amanda's skin, giving it a lustrous, ethereal quality. Her hair tumbled to her shoulders in thick, silvery ribbons. "Trust me," she said.

Anguished sighs wrestled in Winston's throat as he let Amanda take hold of his hand and place it on the smooth curve of her shoulder. A firestorm of passion raged inside him as his fingertips traced the thin strap of Amanda's chemise. Gently Amanda led his hand down to her waist. The cool, sleek silk seemed to dissolve under the heat of his touch.

She's the dean's wife. Winston felt the rise and fall of Amanda's body against him as she breathed. He didn't have to go along with this. He could resist. He could turn on the light and ask Amanda to leave, and that would be the end of it. He could avert disaster. Winston pulled his hand away.

Or he could turn off his spinning mind and follow her lead, hoping the encounter would fill the ever growing gulf inside him.

"Why did you stop?" she breathed into his ear. Taking Winston by the hand once more, she led his palm to the sensuous curve of her hip.

White-hot fire surged inside Winston, scorching the guilt that plagued his conscience. Entangling his fingers in her hair, his burning lips blazed a trail from Amanda's throat to her passionate mouth. Winston's desire was as strong and powerful as a riptide, dragging him violently under. There was no hope of escape.

Chapter Four

Jackson Lowe cut the engine of his 4x4 pickup truck and turned off the headlights. Finding a cigarette in the front pocket of his black T-shirt, he struck a wooden match against his thumbnail and lit it. "Yes, ma'am," he said aloud as swirls of blue smoke escaped the corners of his mouth. "This looks like a fine place to stop for the night."

He'd never been to college, but the idea of it had always fascinated him. In the small area of a college campus there was everything a person could possibly need to live—*except a bar, of course,* Jackson thought. But fortunately those were never *too* hard to come by.

Jumping out of the cab, Jackson wiped a grimy hand across the truck's fender. The once black paint was now covered with a hazy red film of desert dust. The white-and-silver pinstriping, the silver-tipped mud flaps, and even the bank of floodlights on top of the truck had been filthy ever since he'd left Houston.

"I'm sorry, Baby." Jackson sighed, patting the truck's bumper. "I'll get you to a brushless car wash sometime tomorrow. Would you like that?" As a gesture of goodwill he untied the red bandanna from around his neck and wiped Baby's license plate down.

Jackson's black leather cowboy boots sank softly into the ground as he ran up the grassy slope toward campus. It felt good to stretch his legs after a full day of driving. *If I can find me a few vending machines, I've got dinner,* he thought, feeling his pockets for change. He took another puff from his cigarette and shoved the red bandanna into the back pocket of his dirty jeans. It was late, and no one was walking around. He had the whole campus to himself.

"How does it feel to be a college man, Mr. Jackson Lowe?" he asked himself in a deep, formal interviewing voice. "I'd say it feels pretty darn good," Jackson replied in his natural southern drawl. "I think I'm gonna need a drink to celebrate."

Just as the thought of strong whiskey began to tickle his taste buds Jackson heard a giggle coming from a few feet away. *Well, well, what do we have here?* Ducking behind a tree, he saw that it was a woman—a beautiful woman with long blond hair and a sweet face. She was walking with some guy, their arms wrapped around each other. *There goes another one,* Jackson thought, his good mood snuffed out like a match in the wind. He pushed aside a branch to get a closer look at the woman's pretty little face. She looked as sweet as an angel.

I bet you're not as sweet as you look. Gina had seemed sweet too, at first, but eventually she turned into a hideous monster. Just like the rest of them.

Jackson's fingers trembled as the couple walked by. When they were far enough away, he came out from behind the tree and slunk across the grass toward one of the buildings, which was surrounded by a row of hedges. Jackson's heart thumped loudly in his ears and his breathing was heavy. In the dark of night the resemblance was amazing. Instinctively he knew it wasn't her—it *couldn't* have been—but it was close enough.

Silently Jackson watched from the bushes. The couple stopped in the middle of the walkway and the angel turned around so that Jackson could see her golden hair. Then the woman wrapped her arms around the man and pressed her too-willing body against his.

A hot, stabbing pain split through Jackson violently. He'd seen it all before, a year or so ago, standing on his daddy's porch in Texas. Waiting in the middle of the night for his beautiful Gina to come home. *My pure sweet angel. The one I was supposed to marry.* The next-door neighbor Jackson had known since the age of six. The one who was supposed to save herself for him.

Jackson was waiting patiently in the dark for his Gina, just wanting to make sure she got home all right from her night out with some friends. He sat on the porch swing, listening to the dry wind blowing across the desert and thinking about taking a second job so he could buy the engagement ring in time for Christmas. I'm going to get you out of here, Gina, *he thought.*

It was almost midnight when he saw her walking up the dirt road. Jackson was about to wave to her when he saw she wasn't alone. Her arm was curved around Benny Stevenson. They were smiling and laughing and having a great time. Jackson winced, feeling a dull, aching pain as if someone had just socked him in the gut. He hunkered down in the shadows and watched the two of them walk to the front door of Gina's house.

In the porch light Gina's long hair looked like it was made of gold. Her dress was white, as pure and crisp as a wildflower. She was perfect. Benny stood there dumbly, hands at his sides, too stupid to appreciate the innocent beauty before him. But all of a sudden Gina reached up and put her arms around Benny's neck and pressed her mouth against his. They kissed for what seemed like hours, and Jackson watched in horror as his virginal angel transformed into something cheap and dirty. A filthy tramp.

Gina's betrayal sank deep into Jackson's flesh like the fangs of a rattlesnake. The venom hit quickly, a green toxin running through his blood. Jackson stumbled back into his house, drenched in sweat but cold to the bone. He ran into the kitchen and with shaking hands grabbed a long carving knife out of the drawer.

Bleary-eyed and throbbing with pain, Jackson went back outside, but Benny was gone. Gina was opening the door to her house, smiling to herself, unaware of the damage she'd done. Holding the knife behind his back, Jackson walked over to her.

"Jackson," Gina said, startled. "You're up kind of late, aren't you?"

Jackson's breathing was labored, the poison working its way into every fiber, every cell of his body. He shook with rage. "I thought it was supposed to be you and me."

Gina's mouth pinched into a tight line. "I told you already, Jackson, you're a great guy, but I don't think of you that way."

It's the venom talking, *Jackson thought.* He could see it in her eyes. The angel was tainted, spoiled. There was only one way to get the poison out of her. He'd have to bleed it out.

"I'm going to bed now. Good night, Jackson." Gina turned around and was about to open the door when he covered her mouth with his hand.

57

Jackson pulled out the knife, its sleek metal sparkling in the porch light.

Gina screamed, her cries deadened by his powerful hand. She didn't struggle but fell to her knees, her eyes begging for forgiveness.

"Do you know what you've done wrong?" Jackson hissed in her ear, holding the edge of the blade to her throat. "Are you sorry for what you did?" He loosened his hold slightly so she could speak.

"Please, Jackson, I'm so sorry. . . . Please, please don't hurt me. . . . I was wrong. . . . I'm so sorry . . . so sorry," Gina whimpered hysterically. Jackson thought she looked beautiful, white light glowing on her skin. The angel hadn't left her completely. "I won't do it again," she cried.

Jackson smiled, touched by her confession. He held the knife firmly in his grip. "It's too late, Gina. You're tainted, ruined forever. You can't help yourself. I know you'll do it again."

"I won't . . . Jackson, please."

He was calm now, watching her beg with tears of shame running down her face. "I'm gonna save you, Gina," he said soothingly. "I'm gonna set you free."

And with that Jackson drew the knife across her slender white throat. He held her in his arms and rocked her gently, watching as the red venom poured out of her like a river. He watched until her skin turned pale and translucent, until every last drop of poison was gone.

After he set Gina free, he started running. Just got in his truck and left. Jackson thought that would be the end of it, but the more he traveled, the more he was surrounded by angels who'd gone bad. Poison was everywhere. Before he knew it, it had turned into a sport—a hunt for souls.

Jackson spit out his cigarette in disgust, watching the college kids from behind the hedge. "You're no better than the rest of them, you dirty tramp," he muttered through clenched teeth. Revulsion ripped through him like a chain saw as he watched how the girl shamelessly threw herself at the guy. Jackson violently crushed out the cigarette with the heel of his boot. He knew exactly what he had to do.

"Thanks for going to the party for me," Tom Watts said, locking the WSVU doors for the night. "It feels great to finally be caught up at the station. I couldn't have done it without you."

"Anything for my favorite reporter," Elizabeth answered sweetly, taking her boyfriend's arm as they strolled across the empty campus. The hands of the clock tower at the end of the quad were poised just a few minutes before midnight. Most of the students were already asleep, except for a handful of diehards; their desk lights shone through dorm windows, creating luminous dots on the campus landscape.

Tom's eyelids drooped and his arms swung

limply at his sides. "Maybe tonight I'll actually get my first full night of sleep this week," he said, punctuating the sentence with a deep yawn.

"You poor thing!" Elizabeth cooed, running a sympathetic hand through Tom's wavy brown hair. It worried her when he pushed himself to the breaking point for a story. But Elizabeth knew better than to tell Tom to take it easy—she too was guilty of the same crime.

"I like pity," Tom answered with a smirk. "Can I have a little more?"

Elizabeth puckered her lips and wrinkled her brow obligingly. "You poor, poor, sweet darling!" she said dramatically. "Everyone works you to death and they don't appreciate you nearly enough!"

Tom laughed. "You're good at this. . . ."

"Yeah? Well, don't get used to it," Elizabeth answered dryly.

They came to a fork in the narrow paved walkway. Tom's dorm was just a few yards away on the path that veered to the right. Dickenson Hall, where Elizabeth lived, was almost halfway across campus in the opposite direction.

Stopping in her tracks, Elizabeth wrapped her arms around Tom's neck. "Good night," she said dreamily, staring up at him. "I'll see you at breakfast tomorrow."

A puzzled expression darkened Tom's handsome features. "Why are you saying good night now?" he asked. "I still have to walk you back to your dorm."

"I'll walk back by myself. You need to get to bed."

Tom shook his head. "It'll only take fifteen minutes. I want to make sure you get back OK."

Before Tom could protest any further, Elizabeth pressed her fingers gently against his full lips to quiet him. She looked into his eyes, which were now ringed with puffy half circles. "I'll be fine, Tom. You know I can take care of myself."

Tom smiled weakly. "I've never doubted that for a second," he said, kissing her on the forehead. "But walking you home gives me the perfect excuse to spend a little more time with you."

"Not tonight," Elizabeth answered. "You're just going to have to dream about me instead." She tilted back her head and pulled Tom toward her, their lips meeting in a long and lingering kiss.

Tom's strong arms encircled Elizabeth's trim waist and held her close. "If you won't let me walk you home, can I at least convince you to come back to my place to tuck me in?"

Even though Elizabeth was melting in his arms, she held her ground. "I don't think that's such a good idea."

Tom's eyes looked as soft and moist as a puppy dog's as he pouted his lips. "Please?"

"You're a big boy, Tom Watts." She kissed

his pouting lip. "I'm sure you can handle it."

Tom shrugged. "It was worth a try." He squeezed her tightly and gave her one last tender kiss. "Be careful."

"You too." Elizabeth winked at him, then turned down the path. "I'll see you tomorrow."

Heading in the direction of her dorm, Elizabeth hummed contentedly to herself. Up ahead loomed Oakley Hall, dark and silent, where Winston lived. As she followed the hedge-lined path that ran along the building, Elizabeth's euphoria began to fade. He had been acting so strangely on the walk back from the party that she'd felt a little guilty leaving him. He was probably taking the situation with Denise very hard—it was a bad time for him to be alone. *Maybe I should see if he's OK,* Elizabeth thought worriedly. She veered off the path and headed for the main entrance.

Just as she was about to open the front door, she heard a rustling sound. Turning to see where the noise was coming from, Elizabeth suddenly felt a hand reach from behind her and clamp tightly over her mouth. It was a man's hand. *What's happening to me?* she thought frantically. Her heart collided fiercely with her rib cage as she twisted to break free. The attacker pulled her backward, out of the light of the front steps toward the hedgerow. His other hand pinned her wrists behind her back with an iron grip.

"Let me go! Help! Somebody help!" Elizabeth's muted cries met an even tighter grasp. Unable to see anything, she attempted to kick behind her, hoping to nail a shin or a knee. But instead her foot flailed wildly in the air and she lost her balance, falling to the ground. The attacker's hold was firm as he dragged her over the rough pavement.

I've got to do something. A chilling panic gripped Elizabeth as her invisible attacker pulled her into the bushes. She bared her teeth, biting down hard on his palm.

"Stupid girl!" the attacker hissed, yanking his hand away from her mouth. His gravely voice had a southern twang. "You're going to be real sorry you did that to me."

Elizabeth thrashed from side to side but couldn't break free from the stranger's clutches. The hedge ripped her nylons and scraped against her bare legs as he pulled her toward a secluded area. Throwing back her head, Elizabeth drew deep into her lungs for a bloodcurdling scream, but before any sound came out, the attacker held a sharp blade to her throat.

I'm going to die, Elizabeth thought with morbid certainty as the cold, thin metal edge touched her skin. She closed her eyes, waiting for blackness to overtake her. *Please . . . somebody help me.*

*　　　*　　　*

Winston turned on the faucet and splashed his face with cold water for a third time, hoping the sudden, stinging shock would bring him back to reality. Taking a paper towel out of the dispenser, he slowly blotted his face dry. He'd been in the bathroom for at least fifteen minutes—maybe even longer. *Amanda must be long gone by now,* he hoped. He didn't ever want to see her again.

When things had started to heat up between the two of them, Winston freaked out. "No, Amanda—just stop it," he'd said, gently pushing her away.

"What is your problem?" Amanda had folded her arms, looking incredibly annoyed. "You're not having a good time?"

"Of course I am—" Winston shook his head, numbly trying to get the words out. Just the thought of touching Amanda's soft skin made him tremble. And the fact that such a beautiful, worldly woman wanted him certainly didn't make the situation any easier. "I'm not ready for this," he'd said. "And I still love Denise."

Amanda had reached for him, but Winston pulled away again. "I already told you; I can make you forget about Denise."

"I don't *want* to forget about her," Winston had said. "Not yet."

"Come on. . . ." Amanda cooed.

"No!" Winston had shouted. Then he

jumped up and ran to the bathroom before Amanda could stop him.

Look at you. Winston squinted at his disheveled reflection. He was glad he had taken his contacts out—the fuzziness of his vision took the edge off his unbuttoned shirt and messy hair. *Fooling around with the dean's wife.* The words bounced around his head like a pinball. All the excuses in the world couldn't justify what he had done. Winston felt deeply ashamed.

Winston was sure that Amanda would have stormed out, raving mad at the rejection. But when he finally returned to the room, she was still there, sitting on the edge of the windowsill. A growing fear gnawed at his insides. *What is it going to take to get her to leave?*

Winston scratched the top of his head. "I don't think it's a good idea for you to be sitting by the window like that," he said in a meek voice. "Someone might see you."

Amanda didn't turn around. She continued to stare out the window with her back toward him. Was she crying? He couldn't tell.

"Maybe it would be better if you left," Winston said, making a second attempt. He swallowed hard, pushing down the tingling anxiety that was rising in his throat. She'd had way too much to drink. What if she suddenly decided to go home and confess everything to her husband?

Winston stood in the middle of the room,

helplessly waiting for her to do something. He reached for Amanda's trench coat and was about to cover her with it when she suddenly stood up and tugged on the window sash. "Oh no!" she shouted, leaning halfway out the window and looking down at the ground.

Winston's eyes bulged in horror. *She's going to kill herself!* he thought in panic. *I shouldn't have rejected her.* Winston dropped the coat on the floor. "Don't do it, Amanda!" he shouted, lunging for the window, praying he would get there in time. "Please don't jump!"

Jackson felt the familiar, pulsating rush of the knife handle in his hand. His veins pumped pure liquid fire to his head as the disgusting girl struggled for freedom. The power was mind-blowing.

"Are you sorry?" he hissed into her ear. He kicked the backs of her legs and she fell to her knees. "Tell me how sorry you are." He took his hand off her mouth so she could speak.

"Help! Somebody—" She swung her arms blindly in the air. She wasn't sorry.

Jackson clamped his hand over her mouth again and squeezed the delicate bones of her face with such rage that he could imagine her skull crumbling in his grasp.

"You don't deserve to live." Jackson held the tip of the blade just under one ear and was about to draw it across her neck when all of a sudden he heard a rattling sound from above. He looked up and saw that a window three floors above was open. A beautiful woman was glaring down at them. Her blond curls were blown back in the breeze, giving him a good, long look at her face. Their eyes locked for several seconds before she disappeared back into the room.

She's calling the cops. Jackson swore out loud and threw the pathetic girl into the hedge. Before she had a chance to turn around, he was gone.

"Let go of me!" Amanda shouted, pushing Winston away after he pulled her to safety. "I wasn't going to jump!" She yanked him by the arm over to the window and pointed. "That girl down there was just attacked."

Winston blinked a few times to make his eyes focus, but he couldn't see anything. "Where is she?" he asked.

Amanda looked down. "She's gone. The attacker ran away when he saw me. She must've taken off as soon as he let go of her."

Winston's head throbbed as he tried to process the information. "We have to call the police."

"No—we can't," Amanda said, backing away from the window.

Winston stared at her in shock. "Why not?"

"Just think about it. If we call the police, we'll be questioned, and then it will get out that you and I were together." Amanda's big brown eyes bore into him. "We can't let anyone know about us, Winston."

He sat on the edge of his rumpled bed. "It would be terrible if word got out, but think about that poor girl down there. We can't let the guy who attacked her get away."

"She ran off," Amanda reminded him. "I'm sure she's OK. And at this point the guy is long gone—I doubt even the cops could find him." She took Winston's hand and gently stroked his fingers. "So you see, there's no reason to call. The cops would find nothing, and meanwhile our lives would be completely ruined. John would divorce me and you'd lose your job. Who knows, you could even get expelled. It would be pointless."

Winston nodded slowly. Maybe she was right. There had already been too much upheaval in his life over the last few hours; he didn't think he could take much more. Plus he was deeply afraid of hurting Dean Franklin. Amanda was nothing more than a brief, inconsequential fling. A stupid mistake. And he desperately wanted to forget about her.

As Winston fumbled for his glasses, he knocked them down onto the floor and stepped on them with the heel of his dress shoe, shattering the lenses. He shook his head and swore. *Thank goodness I have contacts now,* he thought wearily. *What more could go wrong tonight?*

"I think I'd better go," Amanda said, grabbing her coat. The soft lilt to her voice and the sway in her walk disappeared. The spell had been broken.

Winston offered to walk her safely to the edge of campus. "It's pretty late now," he reasoned. "No one would be out to see us together."

"That would be great—I'm scared to go out there," Amanda said with a hesitant smile. "Can I trust you to keep quiet about what happened tonight?"

"Absolutely," Winston answered before he popped in his contacts and opened the door for her. "There's just as much at stake for me as there is for you."

"I'm glad we understand each other," she said.

But Winston couldn't stop thinking about the girl who had been attacked outside his window. He hoped they were doing the right thing.

Chapter Five

"I was on my way to visit Winston, when all of a sudden this guy jumps out of nowhere and grabs me—" Elizabeth's voice broke into gasping sobs. Her shaking fingertips stroked the raw area where the blade of the knife had grazed her throat. "I thought I was going to die."

Jessica paced their room, her hands balled into tight fists. "When I get my hands on that jerk, he's history!"

Elizabeth reached for another tissue and blew her nose. "He's long gone, Jess. I don't think he was from around here. He had a bit of a southern accent."

"He couldn't have gone too far," Jessica reasoned. Her blue-green eyes were as dark as the Pacific after a storm. "What did he look like?"

"That's the thing," Elizabeth answered,

71

wiping away her tears. "He grabbed me from be-hind—I never saw him. I couldn't even tell you how tall he was." She coughed, and the sensation of hot, painful needles pricked her throat.

Jessica handed her sister a glass of ice water. "Do you think anyone saw the attack? Maybe they could identify the guy."

"I don't know," Elizabeth said gravely as she sipped the cool water. When she was being dragged into the bushes, Elizabeth remembered the alarming feeling of isolation. It was as if the entire campus had fled, leaving her alone with a madman. "He ran away all of a sudden, as if someone had seen him, but after he was gone, no one came to see if I was all right. And no one called the cops. Don't you think that if someone had seen what happened, they would've done something?"

"Any normal person would, but there are a few morons out there who are too afraid to get involved," Jessica said bitterly. "If you ask me, they're just as guilty as the guy who attacked you."

Elizabeth nodded solemnly and nursed her scrapes and bruises with peroxide and a cotton ball. Her knees were still shaking uncontrollably. Why did he attack her? Was it random, or was he after her specifically? If they didn't find the guy who did this to her, Elizabeth didn't think she'd ever feel safe again.

"I guess we'd better call the cops."

Elizabeth sighed. She wasn't in the mood to be questioned. All she wanted was some sleep.

Jessica picked up the phone. "I'll do it for you," she said. "Do you want me to call Tom first?"

Elizabeth knew Tom was going to blame himself for not walking her home, even though she had insisted on going alone. It seemed best to hold off telling him, at least for a little while. "Don't wake him," Elizabeth said.

Jessica dialed the number for the police station. "Yes . . . I'd like to report an attack. . . ."

"Winston, please come in here immediately," Dean Franklin called from his office. "I need to talk to you."

Winston's heart pounded spastically in his chest as he forced himself to his feet. He had spent the better part of the morning avoiding the dean altogether, busying himself with the filing cabinets in the hallway. He carried his heavy conscience with him everywhere, like an enormous boulder chained around his neck.

I wonder if he knows anything. Winston felt an overwhelming sense of dread as he dragged himself into the dean's office. Amanda had made it clear that she wasn't about to say anything to her husband, but John Franklin was a highly intelligent man—he could figure it out.

Winston cleared his throat. "You wanted to see me, sir?" he squeaked.

Dean Franklin dropped the newspaper he was reading. The serious lines that creased his face sent a profound wave of fear through Winston. "Have a seat," he said, pushing the paper aside.

He thinks I was flirting with Amanda by the pool. I just know it. Winston wiped his sweaty palms on the legs of his black jeans. His eyes didn't meet the dean's gaze. At that very moment Winston felt like a medieval criminal waiting for the king to decide his fate.

The dean folded his hands neatly on top of the desk and leaned forward slightly. "So, Winston, did you enjoy yourself at the party?" There was none of the usual warmth in his tone; in fact, Winston was sure he detected a slight hint of accusation.

What should I say? Undoubtedly it was a trick question. Winston's cheeks burned crimson as he mulled over the options. If he said yes, then it would be admitting that he enjoyed being with Amanda—definitely a bad choice. A no answer, on the other hand, might prompt the dean to ask further questions until Winston revealed too much. An equally bad choice.

Winston opted for neutral ground. "It was a nice party," he answered with a reserved smile. His insides twinged as he eyed the gold wedding band on the dean's ring finger.

"I was watching you, Winston," he said. His

graying eyebrows knitted. "I noticed that you spent most of the time talking to my wife."

Beads of sweat trickled down the sides of Winston's face. *I can't take this anymore,* he thought. The tension was more than he could bear. *It was a dumb, stupid, horrible mistake.* Instead of getting himself further entangled in an elaborate web of lies, Winston decided it would be best to come clean and beg the dean's forgiveness.

"You're absolutely right, sir," Winston started slowly. "I did spend too much time with Amanda—"

"There's no need to explain yourself," the dean interrupted. "Amanda told me she enjoyed your company very much."

Winston's hands gripped the arms of the chair, preparing himself for the inevitable shock wave to explode in his face.

Dean Franklin rubbed his temples in slow circles with his fingers. "My only concern was that you didn't talk to any of the trustees. I was hoping you'd make more of an effort to get to know them individually."

Trustees? Winston did a double take. For the first time since he entered the room, he stole a brave glance at his boss. The cold, accusatory expression he thought he had seen on Dean Franklin's face now looked more like exhaustion or even a headache. The dean's eyes weren't vengeful, but concerned. Winston's fear melted away, but his guilt was twice as heavy as before.

"I'm so sorry," Winston apologized, feeling it with his whole heart. The dean might have thought he was talking about the trustees, but for Winston it had a much weightier significance. "I didn't mean to disappoint you."

The dean's mouth curved into a mild grin. "Don't take it so hard," he answered, obviously sensing Winston's intensity. "I'm just asking that you make more of an effort next time—it's nothing to feel bad about."

If only you knew, Winston thought ruefully. His eyes fell to the front page of the newspaper on the corner of the dean's desk. Even turned upside down, the headline was easy to read: SWEET VALLEY WOMAN FOUND DEAD.

"Could you do me a favor?" the dean asked.

"Sure, anything," Winston answered distractedly, his eyes still glued to the newspaper.

The dean took a ten-dollar bill out of his wallet. "Could you run down to the drugstore and get me some aspirin? This headache is absolutely killing me. Arthur Rubble wouldn't leave last night until I let him explain all the ways his chewing gum could benefit the university."

Winston nodded, taking the money. "Do you mind if I borrow your newspaper?"

76

"Go right ahead."

With the newspaper gripped tightly in his hands, Winston headed out of the office and into the bright California sun. Trouble rumbled deep in his gut like an impending earthquake as he read the article over and over again. Just when he and Amanda had seemingly managed to get away with their little rendezvous, a deadly thread threatened to unravel their secret.

"Winnie! Winnie, wait up!" Denise shouted breathlessly as she ran to catch up with him, the soles of her leather sandals slapping against the pavement. "Winston!"

Winston continued walking down the path as if he didn't hear her, his face buried in a newspaper.

Panting, Denise fell into step beside him. "You don't have to stop or anything," she said sarcastically. Winston's face held no reaction. He didn't even look up. Relying on a surefire method to get his attention, Denise threw her arms around Winston's neck and gave him a passionate kiss.

Winston stood stiffly, staring at her, his lips rubbery and unresponsive. Denise pulled away and looked at him, a disturbed glimmer in her blue eyes. "Winnie, what's wrong?"

"Nothing," Winston mumbled, looking away. He continued walking toward the quad.

Is he still mad at me for not going to the party with him? Denise wondered. She sometimes forgot how easily Winston's feelings were bruised and how they took longer than most people's to heal. "I was up most of the night studying," she said pointedly, hoping it would make him feel better. "Aren't you going to ask me how I did on the bio exam?"

"How did you do on the bio exam?" Winston repeated like a robot.

Denise recoiled, feeling slightly hurt herself. "Very well, thank you," she answered testily. "How was the party?"

Instead of looking at her, Winston's eyes remained firmly transfixed on the newspaper. "It was a smashing success," he said in an icy tone. "A rip-roaring good time was had by all."

Denise placed her hand over the paper to get his attention. "Winston, would you look at me?" Winston lifted his head, but his eyes were glazed over, lost in thought, completely unreachable. He had shut himself off and it was starting to scare Denise. "Where are you headed?"

"I'm running an errand for the dean."

"Can it wait? I'd like to go somewhere so we can talk." Denise gently touched his arm, hoping the contact would bring him around. "I'm sorry I bailed on you last night. I want to make it up to you."

Winston moved away from her. "Don't bother," he answered, walking away.

"I just happened to be going by your dorm and I thought I'd drop in to see if you've changed your mind about anything," Amanda said in a sultry voice, walking into Winston's dorm room. She was wearing real clothes this afternoon instead of a chemise, although the low-cut silk blouse and the short black skirt she had on were almost as revealing. Amanda unwrapped an expensive-looking silk scarf from around her head and removed her sunglasses. Free from her disguise, she smiled seductively and leaned toward Winston, as though she were about to kiss him. "Why don't we continue where we left off last night?"

"I *have* changed my mind, Amanda." Winston stepped back instinctively and put the newspaper up as a barrier between them. "I think you'd better take a look at this."

A flash of annoyance flickered in Amanda's eyes as she snatched the paper out of his hands. She scanned the front page, then looked up again at Winston. "Why are you showing me this?"

"I think the murderer was the same guy you saw last night," Winston replied.

Amanda tossed her long blond hair over one shoulder and answered him with a patronizing laugh. "You must be joking, Winston. It says right here that the woman who was murdered was a waitress at a bar—not a college student."

Pacing the floor of his room, Winston was careful not to step within a two-foot radius of the dean's wife. "The murder took place not too far from here, Amanda. After the attacker saw you and left the girl, he probably fled to the nearest place that was still open. In this case, the Dakota Bar and Grill."

"We have no proof that this is the same guy," Amanda insisted, taking a seat on top of the desk.

Winston's patience suddenly snapped. "You told me that you saw a guy dragging a girl into the bushes with a knife to her throat. Less than an hour later, in an empty parking lot about a mile from here, another woman was found stabbed to death. How much more proof do you need?"

The sultry expression on Amanda's face disintegrated. Still, she looked more irritated with him than upset about the murder. "OK, Sherlock Holmes, you proved your point. Is that why you called me over here, to make me feel terrible about not reporting it to the police?"

"No, but I was just hoping you'd change your mind about speaking up," he answered. "It's not too late, you know."

Amanda let out an exasperated sigh. "We've

already been through this, Winston." Her velvety voice was dry and strained. "If I call the cops, my husband, along with the entire city, will find out that you and I were together last night. You said yourself that there was no reason to report the attack."

"That was *before* the murder, Amanda. Because we didn't report the crime, someone died last night." Winston paused, letting the full weight of his words hang in the air. "Maybe your conscience isn't disturbed by that sort of thing, but mine is—I'm going to have to live with this for the rest of my life."

Amanda's pretty face softened as she reached out and placed a consoling hand on Winston's shoulder. "I don't mean to seem so cold, but I have to think of myself here. John and I have built a life together that I just can't afford to lose. You're right, we should've reported the crime last night, but it's too late now. There's nothing we can do."

"The police don't have any leads. The murderer is still on the loose." An icy chill slithered down Winston's spine at the thought of it. "If we don't do something, he could kill again."

"He's probably crossed state lines by now. In that case, there's little we could do," Amanda argued.

A pale ray of midday sun streamed in through the window. Winston leaned against the sill. "What about an anonymous letter?"

Amanda shook her head. "They don't take those kinds of things seriously."

Lifting the sash, Winston leaned his head out the window and peered down at the paved walkway and the hedgerow down below. In his mind's eye he struggled to recall what, if anything, he had personally witnessed. In the daylight, with his contacts, he had no trouble seeing the ground clearly. But it had been dark, and he was terribly nearsighted without his contacts. All that Winston could recall was inky darkness and a fuzzy smudge of light coming from the entrance to the building.

Suddenly Winston had a brilliant idea. He picked up the phone and started to dial the police station.

"What are you doing?" Amanda asked suspiciously.

"Trust me." Winston smiled with reassurance. Then someone came on the line. "Yes, is this the police precinct? I witnessed an attack last night that I think may be linked to the murder near the Dakota Bar and Grill."

Jumping off the desk, Amanda glared at him with daggers in her eyes. *What are you doing?* she mouthed, waving her arms furiously in the air to get his attention.

"Yeah, I'll be here all day," Winston told the dispatcher. "You can send the detectives over at any time." He gave her the address and hung up the phone.

Amanda stalked over to where Winston was standing, her jaw tense. "Are you completely out of your mind? What was that all about?" she demanded.

Unruffled by Amanda's anger, Winston sat down on the edge of the bed, his tense muscles finally beginning to relax. "Don't worry—I'll take care of it. This is the perfect solution."

"You're going to blab everything to the police. That's just perfect," Amanda said snidely as she ground the heel of her leather pump into the floor. "Thanks for ruining my life."

"You don't understand," Winston said coolly. "You're not going to be involved at all. I'm going to pretend to be the witness. I'll be your eyes and ears. I'll see what you saw last night."

The tense corners of Amanda's mouth eased a little. "No one will know that we were together?"

"No one," Winston said firmly. "But in order for this to work, you have to promise you'll tell me absolutely everything you saw," he said solemnly. "I need to know everything."

Amanda shook her head in resignation. "OK, Winston. I promise."

"So tell me, Miss Wakefield, what did this guy look like?" Detective Martin took a seat on top of his metal desk and stared at her with businesslike efficiency. He looked too young to be the chief homicide detective on the force, but the framed award plaques hanging on his office walls seemed to justify his position. His hairline was just beginning to recede and the striped necktie he wore emphasized the solid curve of his belly.

"I don't know," Elizabeth repeated for what seemed like the millionth time while her sister, Jessica, squeezed her hand in support. She looked up at Detective Reese, Martin's younger, sandy-haired partner, hoping at least *he* would listen to what she was saying.

Detective Reese took off his navy blue blazer, revealing the service revolver and brown leather holster strapped to the side of his brawny torso. "What exactly did you see, Miss Wakefield?" he asked, apparently as deaf as his partner.

Elizabeth rolled her eyes. "Nothing," she answered curtly. "Like I told you last night, he came up behind me—I couldn't see a thing."

"Was it someone you knew?" Detective Martin asked, taking out a small notebook from his shirt pocket.

The question was so absurd that both Elizabeth and Jessica fought back fits of nervous laughter. "With all due respect, Detective," Elizabeth said dryly, "if it was someone I knew, don't you think I would've told you that from the very beginning?"

Detective Martin's lips were drawn into a tight, thin line. It was clear that he failed to see the humor in the question. He tried again. "Let me put it this way—was there anything *familiar* about your attacker at all?"

"I don't think so," Elizabeth answered. Her eyelids were hot and stinging from lack of sleep.

Detective Reese rubbed his strong chin thoughtfully. "Didn't you tell us you had a friend who lived in Oakley Hall?"

Elizabeth's blue-green eyes widened. "Yeah, Winston Egbert—but there's no way he'd ever do something like that."

Detective Martin jotted down a few notes. "It's *our* job to eliminate the possibilities, Miss Wakefield."

Jessica and Elizabeth exchanged knowing glances. "I remember specifically that the guy had a southern accent," Elizabeth said. "He probably wasn't from around here."

Reese sipped coffee from a Styrofoam cup. "Do you think you'd be able to work with an artist to come up with a composite sketch of your assailant?"

Visibly irritated, Jessica stood up, her arms folded across her chest. "How many times does she have to tell you? She didn't see a thing—zip, zilch, zero. Leave her alone, OK? She almost got *killed* last night. She's told you everything she knows about a hundred times already!"

Detective Martin's thick black eyebrows raised a fraction of an inch, but the rest of his face remained stony. Elizabeth had a feeling he was just about to ask her another stupid question, but he stopped when a police officer suddenly barged through the door, carrying a clipboard.

"Looks like we finally have a solid lead," the officer announced, showing a sheet of paper to the detectives. "We just got a call from an eyewitness."

"Can I offer you gentlemen something?" Winston asked, inviting the homicide detectives into his dorm room. To Winston's great relief, both men seemed low-key and almost friendly. *This is going to be a piece of cake*, Winston told himself. He only wished he'd thought of the plan last night—before the waitress was murdered.

"Do you have any coffee?" Detective Reese asked, draining the last of his Styrofoam cup.

"Sorry," Winston said with a relaxed laugh. "I've given up caffeine—it makes me too jumpy."

Detective Martin didn't waste any time. He was already taking measurements at the window. "Is this the window where you witnessed the attack last night?"

"Yes," Winston answered with confidence.

He mentally ran down the list of details Amanda had given him to be sure he didn't leave out anything. "I was standing just about where you are right now."

Leaning against Winston's bureau, Detective Reese surveyed the room. "Were you alone last night?"

"Excuse me?" Even though Winston had fully prepared himself for the question, he was still caught a little off guard.

"I said, were you alone last night?"

Winston nodded furiously. "Of c-course," he sputtered. "Completely alone. I was all by myself."

Seconds after the lie tumbled awkwardly from his lips, Winston spotted two very damaging pieces of evidence he'd somehow overlooked. They were the cold, untouched cups of cappuccino Amanda had brought over the night before. And they were two very dangerous inches from Detective Reese's elbow.

How am I going to get rid of the cups without him noticing? Winston felt a cold sweat break over his entire body. If Reese moved his head a little to the right, there was no doubt he'd spot the cups. The detective would instantly know Winston had lied about not drinking coffee, but more important, that he hadn't been alone last night.

Reese shifted his weight, moving within centimeters of spilling the coffee all over the bureau.

Impulsively Winston reached for the toy basketball sitting on top of his laundry basket. "Think fast," he said, tossing it at the detective.

Detective Reese didn't move a muscle and his face remained expressionless as he looked down at the pathetic toy ball bouncing off his chest. "Do you play for the Sweet Valley Peewee team?" he asked humorlessly.

It seemed like the detective was never going to budge. Winston bit down on his bottom lip and tried to think of another ploy. "Shouldn't you be helping your partner out?" he asked boldly, pointing to Detective Martin, who was still taking measurements of the window. "It doesn't seem fair that he has to do all the work by himself."

Detective Reese's sandy eyebrows furrowed and his lips pursed in annoyance. Still he wouldn't move away from the bureau. "Do you have a problem with how I do my job?"

"No—not at all," Winston stammered. *Arguing with the detective is definitely not a brilliant move, Egbert,* he told himself. *But if it gets him away from the coffee cups, then it's worth the trouble.* "I just thought—"

Reese's eyes narrowed. "Maybe you should worry about what you saw last night and leave the investigation—"

"Reese!" Detective Martin broke in. "Stop badgering the witness and get over here!"

In a flash Reese was standing at attention. His sudden movement caused the bureau to rock back and forth on the uneven floor. Winston's heart nearly stopped as he watched the coffee cups knock perilously against each other. As soon as Reese turned his back Winston quietly opened the top drawer of his bureau and carefully put the cups inside.

Detective Martin conferred with his partner, then he turned to Winston, scratching his balding head. "We're going to need a sworn statement from you, Mr. Egbert, detailing everything you witnessed last night. Is there anyone else you can think of who might've seen the attack?"

"I don't think so," Winston answered casually, resting his hands on the top of the bureau and easing the drawer closed with his hip. "As far as I know, I'm the only witness."

Chapter Six

"Why do you need me to come to the station now? I thought I answered all your questions yesterday." Winston spoke into the phone in a hushed voice so that the dean couldn't overhear. Thursday was the busiest day of the week in the office, but there was no reasoning with Detective Martin.

"It's routine, Mr. Egbert," Martin said. "We just need a little clarification on a few of the details. The whole thing will take an hour, tops."

"All right, all right," Winston conceded. "I'll be right over."

After he hung up the phone, Winston slunk over to the dean's desk. *What am I going to tell him?* he asked himself, wringing his damp hands behind his back. There was no way he was going to tell Dean Franklin the truth, but it was going to take a mighty good excuse for him to get out of all the work he had to do.

"Winston, are you all right? You're looking a little pale," Dean Franklin said, looking up from his paperwork.

Winston clutched his stomach—not in an attempt to feign illness but because the gentle, unknowing face of the dean triggered spasms of painful guilt. He felt like a two-faced monster, playing a loyal, conscientious assistant one minute, then a backstabbing traitor the next.

"Yeah—I'm not feeling too well," Winston answered weakly. "I know I have a lot of work to do, but I'd think I'd like to leave—maybe just for an hour or two. I'll try to come back a little later."

The dean smiled compassionately. "If you're worried about the work getting done, please don't. Go home and get some rest, and we'll see how you're doing tomorrow."

Dean Franklin's kindness only worsened the sour feeling in Winston's gut. As Winston headed to the police station, layers of sheer panic topped off the symptoms. *What more could they possibly want from me?* he wondered. After effectively answering the detectives' questions and signing a sworn statement, Winston had been certain that his involvement in the attack was over. But what if he couldn't remember *exactly* what he had said yesterday? What if his stories were inconsistent? Winston's stomach fluttered with the frenetic speed of a humming-bird's wings. The more he worried, the more confused he became about the details.

"Thanks for coming by," Detective Martin said, showing Winston down the stark hallway leading to his office. "I know you're a busy man."

Reese was standing in a corner, sneering at him. Winston sat down. "What's this about?"

"We've rounded up a few suspects that fit the description you gave us of the attacker, and we want you to try to identify him in a lineup," Martin said.

A hard lump formed in Winston's throat. "A lineup?"

"You said you got a good look at the guy," Reese challenged. "So it should be pretty easy for you, right?"

"Right," Winston answered blankly. *A lineup.* Amanda had only given a general description of the attacker—details that could apply to just about anyone. It was hardly enough to go on. "When do you want me to do it?" he asked.

Martin turned and glanced out at the long gray corridor outside his office. "In about ten minutes."

Winston jammed his hands nervously into the pockets of his jeans. "Do you mind if I make a quick phone call?" Instantly an excuse popped into his head. Lying was becoming something he was quite good at. "I have to call my girlfriend—we were supposed to meet for lunch. She'll be worried sick if I don't tell her where I am."

Reese showed Winston to a pay phone in the waiting room. To Winston's dismay, the detective stood nearby and watched while he dropped the coins into the slot. *Please be home,* Winston hoped silently as he dialed the number. The phone rang three times before she finally picked up.

"Hello?"

"Hi, honey—it's me, Winston." He spoke loudly for the detective's benefit.

Amanda was anything but pleasantly surprised. "Winston! Why are you calling me at home? Are you crazy?"

Turning his back to Reese, Winston leaned against the wall and cupped his mouth and the receiver with his hand. "I'm at the police station right now," he answered in a hushed voice. "The detectives want me to pick the guy out of a lineup."

Amanda was silent for a moment. "You should've never gotten involved, you know. This is getting way too complicated."

"I need your help," Winston whispered into the receiver.

"Sorry, big guy—there's no way I'm showing my face at the police station," Amanda protested. "You're on your own with this one."

In his frustration Winston forgot himself,

his voice growing louder. "I'm not asking you to come down here!" He caught himself, looking sheepishly over his shoulder to see if Reese was catching the conversation. The detective's stony glare hadn't changed. "Just give me something more to go on," Winston hushed.

"I told you already—he was Caucasian, tall, probably over six feet, with a lean but muscular build. He had short dark hair," Amanda said. "Maybe he had a tattoo on his right forearm—but I don't know. It was dark. It could've been dirt for all I know."

"Anything else?"

Amanda's voice grew increasingly agitated. "I've told you everything, Winston. I can't help you any more than that."

"If you think really hard, I'm sure you'll—"

"Don't ever call me again," Amanda interrupted. Before he had the chance to ask her another question, she hung up on him.

Winston turned around again and smiled weakly at the detective. "She hung up on me," he said, replacing the receiver on the hook.

Reese suppressed a grin. "I guess your girlfriend takes lunch pretty seriously."

"You should see it when I'm late for dinner," Winston said with forced laughter as the detective led him down the corridor. Despite his casual facade, Winston's nerves were jangling with anxiety.

The room was dark and square, with a few folding chairs and nothing else. Opposite the door was a large one-way mirror, through which Winston saw the lineup room. At the moment it was empty and bare, except for the bright overhead lights and the thick black height lines painted on the back wall.

Detective Martin was already seated off to the side, next to the intercom. "Are you ready, Mr. Egbert?" he asked.

Winston nodded nervously, trying to swallow the lump that still stuck uncomfortably in his throat. Stress tingled in his bones, as if a mild electric current were being passed through them. "What do you want me to do?" he asked.

Reese, who had snagged another cup of coffee, leaned against the door. "Just pick out the guy you saw last night," he said flatly.

But I didn't see anyone last night. Winston's head began to pound.

Detective Martin pressed the intercom button and announced to the security guard that it was time to bring in the suspects. "Take your time, Mr. Egbert," he said mildly, "And remember—you can see them, but they can't see you." Six men walked in single file along the back wall. "Face front," Martin said over the intercom. The suspects turned, every single one of them looking in Winston's direction.

Tall, over six feet. Winston's eyes grazed the

tops of the men's heads, each one easily making it over the six-foot height line. *Lean but muscular build*. Each of the men had varying degrees of lankiness and wiry muscles, but they all fit that description. *Brown hair*. All the way across the board.

The pressure in Winston's head doubled in intensity, as if his head were being squeezed in a vise. Even the men's features were nondescript and frighteningly similar. It was only the little touches that set them apart—one guy wore a black biker jacket, another had sideburns and a striped T-shirt, and the guy on the end wore a red bandanna around his neck and cowboy boots. In spite of the fact that they all looked so similar, Winston thought that at least one of the men had to stick out somehow. Chilling eyes, a nervous tick, a crazed expression. Something had to give the killer away.

"Take a good, long look at each of them," Martin said. "If you need to see a few up close, I can ask them to step forward."

Winston squinted hard, his eyes darting from one suspect to the other. They stood there, tough and silent, giving nothing away. Scratching the top of his head, Winston groaned inwardly. *If I don't pick someone soon, the detectives will start to think I'm a fraud*. Winston's head felt like it was about to explode.

Then Winston noticed something strange

97

about one of the guys. His cheek muscles fluttered ever so slightly. It was a subtle twitch, but nonetheless it was there. To the casual observer, the movement would be virtually undetectable, but Winston was confident in his careful perception. *He's about to crack,* Winston decided with certainty. *I just know it.*

"It's the guy on the end," Winston said, pointing to the suspect on the right. "The one in the leather jacket—it's him."

The detectives exchanged sideways glances, then Martin pressed the intercom button. "Number six, please step forward." Then, turning to Winston, the detective said, "Take a close look—are you certain he's the one?"

"There's no doubt in my mind," he answered, as if he'd never been more sure of anything in his life. The metal studs on the suspect's leather jacket shone harshly under the fluorescent lights. "That's the guy I saw outside my window last night."

Detective Martin sighed deeply and rubbed his high forehead. He pressed the intercom button again. "Let them all go," he announced to the officer.

Winston's eyes narrowed. "Why are you letting them all go?"

Giving him a slap on the back, Detective Reese laughed bitterly. "Once in a while we like to throw in a decoy to make sure our witnesses are credible," he said. "Congratulations, Winston, you just picked Sergeant Robert Mendez—an undercover police officer."

Elizabeth stood waiting outside the lineup identification room, drumming her fingers nervously against the cool concrete walls. On the other side of the gray steel door was the person the detectives said had witnessed her attack. In her right hand she clutched a modest bouquet of wildflowers as a simple thank-you to the person who had the courage to come forward and help nab her attacker. If they somehow managed to get the maniac behind bars, Elizabeth knew she would be indebted to that person for the rest of her life.

What is going on in there? Elizabeth wondered anxiously. She had been waiting outside the room for ten minutes, and who knew how long they had been in there before she arrived. Deep down in her bones, she knew that it had to be a good sign.

Earlier in the day Elizabeth had had her own experience with the lineup. The detectives had brought her into the identification room, even though she still insisted that she hadn't seen anything during the attack. Nevertheless, she took a long look at all six men, hoping to trigger some clue that might have been buried in the back of her brain. Yet nothing came to the surface. She tried to imagine each of them dragging her into the bushes and putting a knife to her throat. But Elizabeth couldn't match a face to the invisible hands that had thrown her to the ground. She simply didn't have enough information to go on, and her conscience wouldn't allow her to accuse an innocent man. After being in the room for less than three minutes, Elizabeth had told the officers to let the men go. Even though it was morally the right thing to do, Elizabeth struggled against it, knowing there was a good chance that the man who'd tried to kill her was in the lineup—and she had set him free.

But the witness seems to be taking much longer than I did, Elizabeth thought with a vague sense of relief. Her heart skipped with cautious joy—every minute that passed increased the odds that her attacker was going to be identified. *Maybe this is the beginning of the end,* she thought wearily. *Soon I won't have to be afraid anymore.*

The heavy steel door creaked open. Detective Martin and Detective Reese stepped out, followed by a shockingly familiar face.

"Winston?" Elizabeth was stunned just to hear herself utter the name. She dropped the bouquet on the tile floor, her eyes widening with astonishment. Martin and Reese continued down the hall without saying a word.

100

"What are you doing here?" she asked.

Looking equally surprised, Winston's jaw fell open slightly. Running his fingers through his dark hair, he squinted at her as though they'd met sometime in the distant past, but he couldn't quite remember when. "I witnessed an attack from my window last night," he answered, retrieving the bouquet and handing it back to her. "What are *you* doing here?"

Elizabeth was taken aback by his question. Didn't he know? "Winston—I was the victim of that attack."

"You?" His eyes nearly popped out of their sockets and his complexion took on an ashen pallor. Elizabeth swore she heard him mutter, "I didn't know it was you," under his breath.

How come he didn't know it was me? Elizabeth thought in confusion. *Didn't the detectives say he saw everything?* "I was walking back from the station that night, and I was thinking about how upset you seemed after the party," she said.

"Was I?"

"I thought so." Elizabeth toyed with the end of her long blond braid, trying not to notice the deep furrows that were appearing on Winston's brow. A strange awkwardness was suddenly wedged between the two of them. "I was walking by your dorm around midnight, and I thought I would stop by to make sure you were all right. That's when the guy

101

jumped out of the bushes and grabbed me."

Winston was quiet as he looked down at the floor. He seemed to be avoiding making eye contact with her. "Did you see what he looked like?"

"No," she answered. "But the detectives said you got a good look at the attacker."

"I thought I did," Winston replied.

"Did the lineup go all right?"

"Not too well," he answered in a tight voice. "I picked an undercover police officer." Winston's eyes glazed over. "I'm really sorry, Liz. I just wanted to help."

"I know you did." Elizabeth tried to hide her disappointment. It seemed odd to her that she was comforting him when she had been the victim. Even though it terrified her to think the attacker was still on the loose, for some reason Winston looked as if he were even more frightened than she was. "These are for you," she said, thrusting the bouquet in his direction. "For coming forward. It was a very courageous thing you did. Thank you."

Holding the flowers limply in his hands, Winston stared down at them. The bouquet shook in his hands. "I don't deserve these," he answered, giving them back to her. "I've got to get going, Liz," he said suddenly. "I'll see you around."

Elizabeth watched Winston run down the hallway, dodging the water fountain and a trash can as though he couldn't get away fast enough. *He's acting even stranger than he did the other night,* she thought. Her mind struggled to put together the bizarre puzzle that was emerging, but she couldn't make the pieces fit. Whatever it was that bothering Winston, Elizabeth was determined to figure it out.

I can't believe it was Elizabeth, Winston thought in shock as he stumbled numbly down the corridor of the police precinct. All the time he'd spent worrying about identifying the attacker, it had never even occurred to him that the victim could be a friend of his. *Elizabeth, of all people—someone I've known practically my whole life.* Winston's stomach caved in as he remembered the look on Elizabeth's face when she told him she was the one who'd been attacked. He had seen the confusion in her eyes when he stared at her in disbelief. *I should've forced Amanda to come forward,* he thought regretfully. *We should've filed a report the night of the attack.*

Winston's chest rose and fell with hoarse, shallow breaths as he came to the end of the hallway. To his right was the men's room. Pushing open the door, Winston brushed his arm across his forehead, wiping away the sweat that was streaming down his face. *The killer is free,* he thought with crushing remorse. *And it's all my fault.*

The rest room door swung closed. The

bland, impersonal beige tiling had a soothing effect on Winston's jangled nerves. The tranquil echo of running faucets drew him inside. *I'll splash some water on my face and try to calm down a little before I figure out what to do next.* There was no point in thinking about things too far ahead—the only thing Winston could do to keep from getting hysterical was to live from moment to moment.

At the end of the wall of white sinks Winston saw a man in jeans and black cowboy boots bent over the basin, splashing his face with water. The man looked agitated as he rubbed his face with paper towels, muttering to his reflection in the mirror. Winston tried not to stare as he turned on the faucets, but he couldn't help noticing how as soon as the man dried off his face, beads of sweat instantly reappeared and dripped down toward the red bandanna tied around his neck. Lowering his head to the sink, Winston cupped his hands under the running water and splashed some on his own face.

This guy sure seems nervous, Winston thought, feeling the bracing chill of the water. Even though the man was all the way on the other side of the bathroom, Winston felt a tense vibe coming off him. Winston splashed water on his face a few more times. The man looked familiar. In the back of his mind he saw the sweating man in a white room with harsh lights and black lines on the walls. He saw five other men lined up next to him against the wall, all of them looking suspicious.

He's one of them, Winston suddenly realized. *He was one of the guys in the lineup.*

Lifting his head, Winston turned off the faucets gingerly, trying not to bring attention to himself. He blotted the water off his face with a paper towel and watched out of the corner of his eye as the man ran his head under the faucet. In the bathroom the man looked grungier than he had in the brightly lit lineup. His nose and chin seemed more angular, with a harder edge. His movements were short and decisive, packed with tension, a hair trigger away from exploding. *There's something definitely frightening about him,* Winston decided.

The man combed back his wet hair, seemingly unaware that Winston was in the bathroom. He unbuttoned his plaid shirt and tied it around his waist. On his right forearm there was a small green tattoo in the shape of a coiled rattlesnake.

Caucasian . . . tall, over six feet . . . lean but muscular . . . brown hair . . . possibly a tattoo on his right forearm. The tattoo. Amanda had seemed so unsure about it that Winston had forgotten about it in the lineup room. But there it was. *I bet he was trying to cover it up with the shirt,* Winston thought. Warning sirens wailed in his head. *This has to be the killer.*

Impulsively Winston splashed his face with water, then grabbed a paper towel and strolled over to the other side of the bathroom, covering his face with the towel as he wiped off the water. He ducked into a graffiti-covered stall, the one right behind where the man was standing, and locked the door. Pressing his face against the gap in the door, Winston silently observed the suspect.

What am I going to do? Winston thought with alarm. *I can't let him go.* But how could he keep him there? He could alert the detectives—but what would he tell them? *"I was confused before, but now I'm sure I've found the guy—he's in the bathroom."* If Winston turned out to be wrong a second time, he would lose his credibility. If he still had any, that was.

In Winston's narrow field of vision he saw the man wipe his face again and loosen the knot in his red bandanna. He grumbled something to the mirror before he turned and headed for the door.

This is it. Winston felt a tingle of anticipation at the base of his spine as he listened to the steady tapping of cowboy boots against the tile floor. In about two seconds the suspect would be out the door, free to kill again.

The bathroom door swung closed with a slow squeak, sending Winston bursting out of the stall. Too many times in his life Winston had failed to make the right decision; too many times he had simply sat back and watched events unfold around him—and it had often caused a world of trouble. But at that moment he knew the cycle had to end. People's lives were at stake now. Even though Winston was acutely aware that he was putting himself in danger, there was no turning back. It was time to take action.

Chapter Seven

"Where's this guy taking me?" Winston wondered aloud as he turned his beat-up VW Bug down a lonely side street. He had been following the suspect's 4x4 truck for what seemed like hours, driving in circles all around town. Luckily the vehicle was big and easy to spot with its yellow floodlights running on top of the cab and the vanity plate that read BABY. He was able to follow at a safe distance without ever losing sight of his target.

Suddenly the truck took an unexpectedly sharp left turn into the narrow back alley parking lot on the edge of town. Winston didn't follow the truck into the lot but pulled over to the side of the road and turned off the car's headlights. A moment later one of the truck's doors opened and the dark figure of the driver hopped out. The glow of his cigarette cut through the gray shadows of dusk.

"Where are you going, cowboy?" Winston wondered aloud, his eyes following the orange pinpoint of light. The suspect casually walked down the side of the street opposite where Winston was parked, bypassing an electronics store, a coin laundry, and a diner. But as soon as the suspect reached the red neon sign of the Gangbusters Saloon, he stopped and went inside.

He went into a bar. Winston slapped his knee, basking in the satisfaction that his hunch had been a pretty good one. The evidence was slowly mounting, and he had a feeling he was definitely on the right track. If he played his cards right, there was a good chance that this man would turn out to be Elizabeth's attacker—and he could catch him himself.

Winston waited a few minutes before entering the busy saloon so the guy wouldn't think he was being followed. Winston had never been in a bar before, but Gangbusters looked a lot like the kind of place he'd seen in Western movies, with its creaky wood floor, low ceiling, loud country tunes pouring from the speakers, and hundreds of liquor bottles lined up against the mirrored back wall.

The bartender was a man roughly in his forties with a faded red T-shirt and a toothpick that he worked between his teeth. He was pouring some sort of clear alcohol into a glass with ice and handing it to the suspect, who sat on a stool in the middle of the bar. There was already an empty glass beside him.

I'm glad this place is busy, Winston thought, taking a seat in a booth near the back of the room. His college sweatshirt and sneakers really made him stand out, but Winston didn't think he'd have too much trouble blending in with so many people around.

"Can I get you something, honey?" a red-headed waitress asked, plopping down a basket of pretzels in front of him.

Remember to blend in, Winston reminded himself. Even though he didn't drink alcohol, Winston imagined it would look suspicious if he ordered a soda. The last thing he wanted was to stand out even more.

"I'll have a scotch on the rocks," he answered, smiling at her as if he'd ordered the drink a thousand times before.

But the waitress wasn't convinced. Her green eyes made a quick appraisal of his SVU sweatshirt. "Do you have any ID?"

Winston stuck his hand in the pretzel basket, and without protest he said, "Just bring me a Shirley Temple."

The waitress laughed and went back to the bar. Winston's gaze returned to the suspect, who threw back his head and drained the rest of his drink. A dark-haired woman in tight jeans and a low-cut shirt had taken a seat next to him, and they seemed to have struck up a conversation—or at least she had. In the smoky distance it seemed to Winston that she was doing most of the talking. All the suspect did was drink and nod every once in a while.

"Shirley Temple," the waitress said, setting down the drink. "That's a buck fifty."

Still looking at the bar, Winston reached into the right pocket of his jeans. It was empty, so he tried his left pocket. It was empty too. Frantically he felt his back pockets.

"I'm sorry," he said with an embarrassed laugh. "I think I left my wallet at home. All I have is a quarter."

The waitress sucked in her cheeks and glared at him. "You ordered something and you don't even have money to pay for it?" she said loudly.

Winston crouched down in the booth. "I'm sorry, I—I—didn't realize—"

"I can't just send the stupid drink back, you know," she snapped, her nostrils flaring. "I have to pay for it out of my own pocket."

"Rachel, is there a problem?" the bartender called from across the room. A few people at the bar turned around to stare. If ever there was a moment when Winston wished the floor would open up and swallow him whole, it was then. Fortunately the suspect was already hunched over his third drink, too busy to notice.

"It's nothing I can't handle, Walter," Rachel said, taking the drink back. She bared her teeth at Winston, who was cowering in his seat. "I think you'd better be on your way."

Winston nodded. When he nervously reached for another pretzel, Rachel yanked the basket away and stalked back to the bar. Discouraged beyond belief, Winston looked up to see that the suspect had suddenly turned his attention away from his drink and the gabby woman beside him and was staring at a blond woman with a square face who was passionately kissing her boyfriend in the corner. The look on the suspect's face was so chilling, it made Winston's blood freeze.

I can't leave now, Winston thought. *Things are just starting to get interesting*. He crouched down in the booth, hoping no one would notice if he stayed just a little longer.

"Excuse me—are you expecting anyone?" A short man in a white cowboy hat appeared, staring strangely at Winston slouching in the booth. A guy who looked like the man's brother was standing behind him, along with what appeared to be their dates.

"No," Winston murmured, not turning away from the drama unfolding at the bar. The suspect's eyes were still glued to the couple as he downed a fresh drink.

"Then do you mind if we sit here? There's not enough room for four at the bar," the man said, tipping the brim of his hat.

There was no way Winston was about to give up his prime seat, especially now. He was just too close. "Sorry—it's first come, first served."

The man's face turned a dark purple-red color, while the other three frowned at Winston in disapproval. "Rachel? Can you come over here a minute?" the man said.

Oh no, Winston thought, *he knows the waitress.* Before Rachel had time to reach the booth, Winston was already on his feet, bounding toward the pay phone in the back of the room. Obviously he couldn't stick around to see what the suspect was about to do. He had to come up with an alternate plan. And fast.

The commotion behind him was growing louder as Winston dropped his only quarter into the slot. With superhuman speed he dialed a number and just as he heard someone pick up on the other end, Winston saw the bartender coming at him, the blue veins in his neck bulging.

Winston had no idea who answered the phone, but that was a chance he was willing to take. "Meet me at the Gangbusters Saloon parking lot in five minutes," he shouted into the receiver just seconds before he was thrown out the back door.

*   *   *

"Winston has been impossible to get ahold of lately," Denise said, squirting ketchup on her snack bar veggie burger. She'd spent all evening looking for Winston and had inadvertently missed dinner in the dining hall. "I think he's trying to get back at me for house-sitting—I don't know. I'm sorry if this is wrecking your plans."

"It's no problem at all, Denise," Bruce said with a smile as he cracked open a can of soda. "When Lila's out of town, I'm a free man. Just say the word and I'm here for you."

Denise blushed. "I can't tell you how much this means to me."

"The pleasure's all mine," Bruce said with a smug grin.

"I'm sure it is," Denise teased. She bit into the burger, suddenly realizing just how hungry she really was. Anytime there was a disruption in her life, it had a way of throwing off Denise's body completely, and for the past week she'd had an incredibly tough time sleeping even though she was exhausted, eating even though she was famished, and concentrating when she had to study. *I can't wait until this is all over,* she thought.

"Is tomorrow OK?" she asked.

Bruce nodded, stealing a fry from her plate. "Do you think you'll be able to get in touch with him?"

115

"I don't know," Denise answered, dabbing the corners of her mouth with a napkin. "He's not answering any of my messages."

A thoughtful look came over Bruce's handsome face. "I could call him if you want."

"Would you?"

"Sure," Bruce said casually. He stretched his arm across the back of the booth. "I'll just tell him to meet me by the coffeehouse. I'll tell him there's something important I need to talk to him about."

Denise reached across the table and touched Bruce's arm appreciatively. "That'll definitely work. Thanks so much." She smiled as Bruce gave her a wink.

Moments later Jessica came sidling up to the table and slid into the seat next to Denise. "Hey, guys," she said, pouting her lips. Denise had seen that look before—it meant that Jessica had important news.

"How's Elizabeth doing?" Denise asked right away. Even though she'd been preoccupied with thoughts of Winston, Denise still couldn't get Elizabeth's attack out of her mind. "Is she all right?"

"She's still a little shaken up, but who wouldn't be?" Jessica flashed a look of disgust in Bruce's direction, but he didn't seem to notice. "How's Winston?"

Denise threw her hands up in the air. "I

wish I knew. I've been trying to find him all day. Have you seen him?"

Jessica shook her golden blond head. "Nope, but Elizabeth did—at the police station."

"The police station?" Denise and Bruce said in unison. A heavy feeling of dread was starting to creep up on Denise. "What was he doing there?"

Jessica arched one eyebrow in disbelief. "Don't you know?" She shot a second nasty look at Bruce. "He is your *boyfriend,* after all."

"We haven't spoken to each other much lately," Denise answered in an annoyed tone. "What's going on?"

A slight smirk curled Jessica's lips as she took a dramatic pause. "It seems that Winston is the only person who witnessed Elizabeth's attack the other night."

Amanda opened the passenger-side door of Winston's parked car and slithered inside. Her hair was pinned up in a French twist and her lips were meticulously painted the color of rubies. From the moment she got into the car, Winston expected her to start screaming at him for calling her again. But instead she looked at him with an enormous smile on her face.

"I didn't think you'd make it," Winston said uneasily, his pulse quickening. His reason for calling her was legitimate, but Amanda's sexy smile still made him feel guilty.

Amanda crossed her long legs and kicked off her strappy sandals, revealing her pretty feet and toenails painted the color of rubies. The sheer floral dress she was wearing reached well above her knees. "Obviously you've figured out what it takes to make me respond," she said in a husky tone. She tickled his earlobe. "When you called earlier and said to meet you at the police station—that would never work on me. But a mysterious phone call telling me to meet you right away in a bar parking lot—the temptation was too much. I just couldn't keep myself away."

Winston inched away from her toward his door, ignoring the delicious spark of her touch against his skin. "It wasn't a trick," he insisted, clearing his throat. "One of the suspects is in that bar right now, and when he comes out, I want you to tell me if he's the guy you saw from my window."

"Stop playing games, Winston." Amanda moved close enough to press her leg against his, causing Winston to squirm. "You're just using this 'suspect' thing as an excuse to see me again." She put her hand on his knee.

"No, I'm not," Winston faltered. The clean, peachy scent of Amanda's perfume flooded the car and wrapped itself around him like a noose. She breathed softly in his ear. Winston edged away, flattening himself against the door. "Trust me— this is serious. I'm not doing this to see you."

Amanda laughed. "You don't have to be embarrassed, Winston. I know you're sorry you pushed me away the other night. We can pick things up right where we left off." Her fingertips caressed his shoulders and she moved in closer still, until there was nowhere left for Winston to go. Her ruby red lips kissed his neck, making a path to Winston's mouth. He felt his solar plexus dissolving, right along with the willpower he'd thought he had. Just as his lips parted to kiss hers, out of the corner of his eye Winston saw something move.

"It's him!" he said quickly, turning his head away from Amanda's seductive mouth. "The guy is coming out of the bar. Do you see him? Is he the one?"

As if she didn't hear, Amanda kissed him even more amorously, sending a disturbing shiver through Winston's body.

"Amanda! Amanda!" Winston protested between kisses. He knocked his head a few times against the window glass in an attempt to get away from her. "Just hold on a minute—is he the guy?"

An exasperated sigh escaped from Amanda. "Who do you want me to look at?"

Winston pointed to the man, who was now walking down the sidewalk. His tall, wiry frame moved with languid purpose, and a glowing cigarette dangled from his lips. "The guy right there!" Winston said.

"How should I know if he was the one?" Amanda said with a dismissive wave. "It was dark."

The suspect crushed out his cigarette and scratched at the red bandanna around his neck as he walked toward his truck. He lifted his black T-shirt above the waistband of his jeans and reached for something near his hip. That was when Winston saw the hunting knife pouch hanging from his leather belt. Panicking, he followed the suspect's gaze to see a couple walking just a few yards away from him—the same couple who had been kissing in the corner of the bar.

Something was going to happen. Winston could feel it in his blood. "Please—just take a close look," he said with urgency. "It's important."

But Amanda wouldn't listen. She grabbed Winston's face and planted a huge kiss on his mouth. Winston struggled to get free, his head rolling against the window. Finally, in a desperate effort to get her attention, he reached behind his back and yanked on the door handle. The car door swung open and they both tumbled out onto the pavement.

"Look what you've done!" Amanda hissed, showing him the dirt that streaked her dress. She climbed back into the car and sat in the driver's seat, trying to rub out the stain. "What's wrong with you?"

Winston stared up at her from the blacktop.

"You weren't listening to me!" A truck engine rumbled in the distance. Winston scurried to his feet. "Move over! I have to follow this guy!"

Amanda shook her head, refusing to move. "It's obvious that you're too immature to handle an adult relationship."

"We don't *have* a relationship. Our night together was a mistake. You're a married woman and I've got Denise—" Winston stopped short when remembered that Denise wasn't exactly his girlfriend anymore. "I'm sorry I let anything happen between us," he finished angrily. When Winston looked up, he saw the truck pulling out of the parking lot. "Now if you'll please move over, we'll talk about this later."

"We're not going to talk about this because it's over!" Amanda shrilled. She swung her scraped legs around and got out of the car, holding her head high in the air. "I thought you were a man, Winston, but I can see that you're nothing but a little boy."

Ignoring Amanda's tantrum, Winston jumped into the driver's seat and poised his foot on the accelerator, ready to take off. He tried to locate the truck, but it was already gone. During Amanda's fit the suspect had slipped away into the night. Winston smacked the steering wheel with his hands and rested his head on his arms in defeat.

"And let me tell you something else,

Winston," Amanda said with an icy edge, oblivious to the gravity of the situation around her. "I'm the best you'll ever get."

Jackson pulled off into a wooded area, hungry for the sight of blood. The woman he had seen in the bar had just said good night to the man she had been kissing so passionately and was walking along the dirt road by herself. *I'm not going to get caught this time,* Jackson promised himself. He jumped out of his truck and sniffed the clean air. It was a good night for hunting.

A good hunter needs the right kind of hunting equipment, Jackson thought as he reached into the cab of his truck and pulled the bench seat forward. He yanked down the vinyl flap that covered the back of the seat and grinned at the carefully sorted collection of knives he kept hidden there. Each blade had its own purpose, its own meaning. But the most special of all was the gleaming carving knife he had taken on the night he saved Gina. It was the most precious piece in the collection.

"Let's see . . . which one will it be tonight?" Jackson ran his fingers across the blades, each hanging by a magnetic strip he'd glued to the back of the seat. He looked over at the woman, who was walking farther and farther away from him, her white-blond hair illuminated by the moon.

From the way she'd thrown herself so shamelessly at that man in the bar, Jackson had a feeling that it had been a long time since she had been pure. The poison was deep in her system—so deep, he wasn't sure if there was anything left to save. But if they weren't worth saving, then they didn't deserve to live either.

Worthless piece of trash. Jackson spit on the ground. The tension in his muscles was building with each wave of fury that broke over him. Hate seethed beneath the surface of his skin like molten lava, ready to erupt. Every woman he encountered was tainted, spoiled, rotten—it was beginning to dawn on Jackson that he might never be able to settle down and have a family because of it. Gina ruined his life. They all did. And he was going to make sure that they paid for it.

And now it's your turn, he said to the shadowy figure at the end of the road. Jackson took out the dagger in his leather pouch and replaced it with a long blade that had a jagged edge near the top. The bitter, red snake venom was flowing through his system at lightning speed as he closed the truck door with a quiet but satisfying click. Then Jackson headed down the road on foot, ready to meet his next victim.

Chapter
Eight

Before Winston even opened his eyes on Friday morning, he knew it was going to be a terrible day. Under the warmth and security of his blankets he could feel the damp chill of doom hovering over him like a dark thundercloud. In a few short days Winston had somehow managed to attract trouble like a wet dog at a flea convention. And the sharp burning in the pit of his stomach told him that his problems were far from over.

There's no way I can make it to class today, Winston thought miserably as he rolled over and pushed aside the pillow that was covering his head. The thin gray light that trickled into his room was hardly inviting, especially considering his state of mind. He couldn't think of anything that could possibly motivate him to get out of bed. As far as he was concerned, he could spend the rest of his life there.

The countless reasons for Winston's depression surged through his brain. *Where do I begin?* he thought sadly. *Not only was one of my best friends attacked, but because of my stupidity, a murderer is on the loose. The police think I'm a total idiot, and the one person who could crack the case not only doesn't care but is also the dean's wife, who I just happened to . . .*

Winston knew it was pointless to beat himself up over his missteps. But even with the overwhelming number of horrible and bizarre things that had been happening to him over the last few days, there was one that hurt him more deeply than any of the others. Winston missed Denise more than anything, and it left an aching hollowness inside him. His biggest regret about the whole mess was that he just stood back and let Bruce take her away from him. Winston wished he had fought for her instead.

Reaching out from under the covers, Winston groped blindly for the TV remote on his nightstand. Holding the remote high above his drowsy head, he aimed at the small color TV on the bookshelf just opposite his bed. A day of watching television was the perfect anesthetic to dull the wrenching pain in his heart.

"This morning we have mostly cloudy skies, with a ninety percent chance of rain this afternoon," the TV weatherman chirped. "It's the perfect day to stay in bed if you can."

"I agree completely," Winston said to the TV as he rubbed the sleep from his eyes. He was starting to feel better already.

"Thanks, Stormy," the anchorwoman said. "Now for today's top story—a second Sweet Valley woman has been found stabbed to death, this time in a secluded area less than a half mile from the Gangbusters Saloon, where she was last seen. . . ."

Throwing off the blankets in a frenzy, Winston leaped out of bed and stood close to the screen. The TV showed a picture of the victim, a smiling blond woman with a square face. It was the same woman Winston had seen at the bar with her boyfriend. She was the one the suspect had stared at so coldly—the same one who left the bar at almost the same time he had.

"So far, the police have no leads. They're asking anyone with any information at all pertaining to the case to please contact the station immediately," the newswoman said.

Without a moment's hesitation Winston popped in his contacts and threw on a pair of dirty jeans and a brown plaid shirt that had been draped over his desk chair. Grabbing his car keys, he ran out the door and began rehearsing exactly what he was going to say once he got to the police station, just in case the detectives got suspicious.

*   *   *

"Why couldn't you identify him in the lineup?" Detective Martin asked after Winston explained what had happened the night before. The detective closed the door to his office, wrinkled his eyebrows skeptically, and approached Winston from the left.

In the reflection of one of the detective's award plaques Winston saw that his unwashed hair was standing on end. He patted his hair in an attempt to flatten it and tried to forget how ridiculous he looked. "The lights threw me off," he said defensively. "They were too bright."

"So you see better in the dark? Is that what you're saying?" Detective Reese challenged. He came at Winston from the right, rolling up his shirtsleeves as if he were planning to arm wrestle him for the truth.

With detectives on either side of him, Winston felt claustrophobic. "Not at all. It's just that the bathroom lights were dimmer, like the light coming from the front of my dorm on the night of the attack. When I saw how nervous he was, that made me even more suspicious."

"But are you *sure* it's him?" Martin asked.

"Yes." Winston nodded. "I'm positive this time."

"So you followed the guy to Gangbusters?" Martin asked a moment later.

Winston exhaled loudly. "Yeah."

Reese rubbed his smooth chin thoughtfully. "Why didn't you tell us sooner and save yourself the trouble?"

"I wanted to be one hundred percent sure—no mistakes this time." Winston's eyes shifted from one detective to the other as if he were watching a tennis match. "Then when I saw the news this morning, there was absolutely no doubt in my mind that he was the right guy."

Detective Martin walked around to the back of his messy desk and took out a notepad. The room was quiet as he jotted down a few notes, and Winston suddenly became acutely aware of the sounds in the room. The scratching of Martin's pen against paper, the buzzing of the overhead lights, the heavy sound of Reese breathing over him—but none of these sounds were as loud as the thumping of Winston's heartbeat as it echoed in his ears.

Reese put a strong hand on the back of Winston's chair, tilting the front legs off the floor slightly. "What did the guy do in the bar?"

"He drank a lot," Winston answered. For once it was nice to talk about events he really had witnessed instead of trying to explain what someone else had experienced. "I remember he kept staring at this one woman the whole time—she was the same one who was found murdered. I saw her picture on TV."

Martin's thick eyebrows raised slightly.

"You said you saw the suspect leave the bar about an hour after he arrived?"

"That's right."

"Then what?" Martin asked.

Winston shook his tousled head. "I don't know."

Reese let go of the back of Winston's chair, and the front legs slammed against the floor. "Didn't you continue to follow the suspect at this point?"

"Aman—" Winston stopped short, suddenly realizing in panic that he was about to tell them that he was with the dean's wife. He quickly corrected himself. "I mean, *the* man jumped in his truck and tore out of the parking lot so fast, I couldn't keep up with him."

"You couldn't keep up," Martin repeated, writing it down.

"Exactly," Winston answered. He gave them a detailed description of the truck, right down to the license plate.

When Detective Martin finished taking notes, he extended his hand to Winston. "The information you gave should be sufficient for a search warrant. Thanks for your help, Mr. Egbert. You're free to go."

Winston shook the detective's hand gratefully, feeling as though a weight had suddenly been lifted from his shoulders. "That's it? I don't have to testify?"

Martin closed his notebook. "Not unless you witness a murder."

"Who is it?" Elizabeth said in a tough-sounding voice. She got up from her desk and grabbed one of her sister's shoes, holding it high above her head with the four-inch spike heel pointing out like a weapon.

"Detectives Martin and Reese—may we come in?"

With the shoe still firmly in her grasp, Elizabeth unlocked the two new dead bolts she had installed, leaving the door chain in place. She opened the door a crack.

"Can I see some ID, please?" Elizabeth said.

The detective thrust a gold badge through the crack in the door. Elizabeth examined it carefully before letting Martin and Reese inside—since the attack she wasn't about to take any chances.

"Did we catch you at a bad time?" Martin asked, eyeing the spike-heeled shoe in her hand.

Elizabeth felt her face grow hot with embarrassment. She tossed the shoe back where she found it—on Jessica's desk. "Not at all," she said with a nervous laugh. "I'm still feeling a bit tense."

"That's completely understandable," Reese said with a boyish grin. "But we have some news that might make you feel better."

"What is it?"

Detective Martin took a seat on the couch. "Your friend Mr. Egbert came to us with a positive ID earlier today." The detective explained how Winston tracked down the suspect.

"That's great!" Elizabeth said, feeling as if the wind had just been knocked out of her. "Did you make an arrest?"

"Not yet," Reese answered. "Winston gave us enough info to get a warrant. We searched the suspect's truck and traced him to a hotel room about five miles from here, but we didn't turn up anything."

Elizabeth's face fell as she sank into a nearby chair. "Now what?"

"The most important thing is to get this guy off the street," Detective Martin said, resting his folded hands on his broad belly. "So we'd like to charge him with assault for now— if that's the only way we can get him."

Even though she never saw his face, the idea of confronting her attacker in court sent a horrified shiver down Elizabeth's spine. "How can I testify? I didn't see anything—"

"Don't worry about a thing, Miss Wakefield," Detective Martin said in a confident tone. "Your friend Mr. Egbert is going to be the star witness."

Winston walked across campus, carrying his history book and whistling to himself. As soon as he returned from the police station he decided to go to his classes after all. Things were looking up. Now that he was no longer involved in the police investigation, life had become much simpler. Not only could he stop lying about what he saw the night of the attack, but he also had no reason ever to contact Amanda again. The only thing left to return his life to normal would be if Denise came back to him.

It had stopped raining, and the sun was trying to break through the clouds. As Winston ran up the steps to the history building he suddenly heard his name being called from a few feet away. Turning around, he spotted two men in matching gray overcoats standing at the base of the steps—Martin and Reese.

Oh no—what now? Winston thought.

Detective Reese approached him. "Mr. Egbert, may we speak with you for a moment?"

Winston's shoulders slumped and his arms swung limply as he slowly descended the stairs. With each step he took, his spirits sank lower and lower.

"What is it?" Winston asked, immediately flanked on either side by the detectives.

Reese pulled a pair of gold-rimmed sunglasses out of his overcoat pocket and put them on, looking up at the break in the clouds. "The warrant didn't turn up anything," he said crisply.

I don't like where this is headed. Winston started to walk along the path, and the detectives fell into step beside him. "I'm sorry," he said, shaking his head. "But I've done all I can."

"There's no chance of getting the guy on murder charges, but we might be able to get him for assault," Martin said cautiously. "Only with your help, of course."

Winston swallowed hard. "What kind of help?"

Detective Martin rested his hand on Winston's shoulder. "You're going to be our star witness at the assault trial."

Winston stopped in his tracks. His stomach plummeted like a runaway elevator car. "I thought you said I didn't have to testify."

"That was when we thought the warrant was going to provide us with some evidence," Reese said, running a hand through his sandy hair. "But it didn't."

It took a few moments for the full impact of the detectives' words to sink in, but once Winston had absorbed it all, his future passed through his mind like a psychic vision. Winston saw Denise, Dean Franklin, Elizabeth, his parents—everybody—finding out about his fling with Amanda. Everyone would despise him. Elizabeth would think he was a jerk, Dean Franklin would expel him from school, his parents would be disappointed, and Denise would never speak to him again. It would be like sentencing himself to life in prison.

"I can't do it," Winston answered simply.

"What do you mean, you can't do it?" Reese said, his voice edgy. "What's the problem? You saw the guy, didn't you?"

"Of course I saw him!" Winston shouted back. The muscles in his shoulders tied themselves into ropy knots as the stress kept on building. "I can't do it—that's all."

Martin patted Winston gently on the back, as if he understood everything. "I can imagine what you're going through, Winston. Testifying can be scary. But this is serious business. We've got what appears to be a serial killer on our hands. He's running around Sweet Valley just waiting to prey on the next young woman who crosses his path," he said. "Do you have a girlfriend, Winston?"

I used to, he thought bitterly, but he nodded anyway.

"Imagine if this animal gets his hands on your girlfriend; someone witnesses the attack, but refuses to come forward. How would you feel?"

Winston already knew the answer to that one without giving it a second thought. "I'd be totally devastated."

"Understandably so." Martin nodded. "Now think for a moment about the families of the victims. How do you think they feel?"

That was the last thing Winston wanted to think about. Martin was wearing him down, beating guilt into him like a hammer, splintering every bit of Winston's conscience. He couldn't stand it any longer. "What do you want me to do?"

"The hearing is in a few days," Reese said matter-of-factly. "If we can present enough evidence, it'll go to trial. In the meantime we need you to meet with the district attorney so he can prepare the case."

Martin gave Winston a reserved smile. "I'm proud of you, Winston," he said, patting him on the back. "You're doing the right thing."

Reese nodded. "It'll be a cinch," he said. "All you have to do is tell the judge what you saw."

That's the problem, Winston thought. *I didn't see anything.*

Chapter Nine

"What do you mean, you're going to testify?" Amanda shrilled as she took a seat next to Winston on the bleachers surrounding the athletics fields.

An hour before, when he had called to tell her the news, she demanded to see him immediately. Winston had agreed to meet her only under the condition that it was in a public place so he could maintain some control of the situation. And of himself.

"I can't believe you're going to do this to me, Winston," she shouted.

"The detectives were persistent," Winston answered calmly, looking around the deserted lacrosse field. To his relief, no one was around to hear Amanda raving. "I didn't have much choice. We've got to put the guy behind bars—he's dangerous."

"They're going to find out about us, you know." Amanda closed her eyes and drew her pale lips into a tight frown. Fine lines appeared around her mouth, making her look even older than she was. "This hearing is going to ruin my marriage."

Winston clenched his teeth. "Maybe that's something you should've thought about before you came on to me," he said with a biting tone.

Amanda laughed bitterly, tilting her face up to the harsh sunlight, leaving Winston wondering why he had found her so attractive a few days ago. "You're just an immature college kid," she said acerbically. "What would you know?"

"I know that you have a beautiful house and a successful husband who adores you," Winston said evenly.

Amanda's face fell. "I assure you it's not all as glorious as it seems." Tears softened her brown eyes. "John and I had an affair while I was a student at UCLA—he was a professor there at the time. We were very discreet about our relationship. No one on campus knew about it, but somehow his wife found out. John tried to break it off with me, but I can be pretty persuasive when I set my mind to something."

Winston nodded. He knew all too well about Amanda's powers of persuasion.

"Finally I convinced him to leave his family," she continued through a sudden wave of tears. "I was thrilled at first. We got married and moved to Sweet Valley as soon as I graduated and John got this great job as dean—everything was perfect. But it didn't take me long to realize how lonely life could be for a dean's wife." She paused for a moment to catch her breath. "He's always busy with some sort of business. And since I'm at least twenty years younger than the other college administrators' wives, they want nothing to do with me."

Amanda's sob story had no impact on Winston whatsoever. He sat there quietly, listening, feeling neither pity nor anger. It was clear to him that Amanda had created her own problems and that she had no one to blame for her misery but herself.

"Did you ever tell him you were unhappy?" Winston asked.

Amanda pulled a tissue out of her expensive leather purse and dabbed the corners of her eyes. "I tried, Winston—I really did. But it was so hard. John had given up his family for me, and it just didn't seem right to complain. His first wife had never been very supportive, and I didn't want him to think I was going to be like her." Sniffling, she twirled a fat blond curl around her finger. "The next thing I know, I'm meeting one of John's students—a cute young guy who's really nice to me—and I suddenly find myself uncontrollably attracted to him."

Winston's face reddened and he looked

away. "I'm really flattered, Amanda, but I had no intention of ruining your life."

"I wasn't talking about *you*, Winston," she said with a nasty laugh. "You're hardly the first student I've gotten involved with."

Winston shot her a look of contempt and nursed his deflated ego. "Look—I don't want to get into your personal life. The point is that I have to testify at the hearing and I need your help."

"This is the closest I've ever come to being found out, and it scares me," Amanda whimpered as black streaks of mascara coursed down her face. "This is the first time I've ever realized how much I could lose."

"Yeah, like your big house with the swimming pool," Winston said sarcastically.

Amanda wiped her flushed cheeks with the back of her well-manicured hand. "I know I mean absolutely nothing to you, but think about John. I know you respect him. If he found out about us, it would ruin his life."

Winston took a deep breath. "The last thing I want is for Dean Franklin to find out," he said. "But I still have to testify."

"I'll do anything you ask," Amanda said desperately. "If there's anything you want, I can get it for you. Just as long as you don't testify."

Balling his hands into tight fists, Winston was determined to hold his ground. "When I go into that courtroom in a few days, I'm going to have the impossible job of convincing a judge I witnessed an attack I know nothing about. Without your help there's a good chance they're going to think I'm a fraud—they're going to start asking questions, and *I'll* be the one on trial. But if you agree to help me, there's a chance the attacker will be put away. Then we'll be able to put this mess behind us for good."

Amanda fell silent for several minutes. "I'll do it only if you promise me that no one will discover our secret."

"I can't promise anything," Winston answered honestly. "But I'll do everything I can to make sure it doesn't happen."

"You'd better," Amanda said darkly, her face taking on a hard edge. "Because if I go down, I'm taking you with me."

"We have a solid team lined up this year," said Shawna Rowley, captain of the SVU women's lacrosse team. She smiled broadly into the video camera. "We're looking forward to a great season."

"Well, we look forward to watching you out on the field," Elizabeth said, speaking into the microphone. She looked into the camera lens and flashed her most professional, journalistic smile. "For WSVU, I'm Elizabeth Wakefield, reporting from the campus athletics complex."

"And that's a wrap!" Tom announced, taking

the camera off his shoulder. "Thanks for the interview, Shawna. That's going to make a nice piece."

Shawna zipped up her windbreaker and grabbed her gym bag. "It was nice meeting you two. I hope to see you at the games."

Elizabeth wound the microphone cord around her arm. "We'll definitely be there," she said, waving good-bye as Shawna headed into the locker room.

"Do you think we can get this edited by dinnertime?" Tom asked, packing up the rest of the equipment.

"I don't see why not," Elizabeth answered optimistically, even though she knew it was going to be a tough job. Tom could have asked her if she thought they'd be able to jog across the country in time to see the sun set in New York, and she probably would have given him the same answer. Now that Winston had positively identified her attacker, anything seemed possible.

When they finally gathered up their things, Tom headed for the back door. "Let's cut across the lacrosse field. It's a lot shorter that way."

Elizabeth followed Tom as they walked out into the sunshine. Her mood was as light as the breeze that blew across the playing fields. Glancing up at the empty bleachers, she caught a glimpse of the person responsible for her good mood—Winston himself, hanging out in the stands.

"Hi, Winston!" Elizabeth shouted. He was talking to someone she couldn't see. She repeated his name again, but he didn't seem to hear her. "Go on ahead to the station," she said to Tom. "I want to thank Winston for helping to catch the guy who attacked me."

Tom frowned. "I'll wait," he said solemnly. "I'm not crazy about letting you walk by yourself, considering what happened last time."

"Don't be silly—it's broad daylight," Elizabeth insisted.

"I'm not going to feel secure until that guy's in prison," Tom said.

Elizabeth kissed him tenderly on the forehead. "If it makes you feel any better, I'll have Winston walk me back to the station, OK? Now go on ahead—we have a deadline."

A reluctant smile played on Tom's lips as he crossed the field without her. "If you're not back in fifteen minutes, I'm sending out a search party!"

"Wait at least twenty before you alert the National Guard!" she called back to him.

Elizabeth jogged around the perimeter of the field, anxious to talk to Winston about his ordeal at the bar the night before. She was touched that he was putting himself in such a dangerous position for her, especially after his strange behavior when she had seen him outside the lineup room at the police precinct. In retrospect, Elizabeth

143

decided that it was probably just a case of bad nerves that made him act that way. The important thing was that he finally found the attacker and that he'd be going to trial.

When she nearly reached the section of bleachers where Winston was sitting, Elizabeth slowed down. Shielding her eyes from the sun, she looked up at the very top of the bleachers. Elizabeth was about to call his name once again, but she stopped short when suddenly she realized that Winston was talking to Amanda Franklin, the dean's wife.

Why is he talking to her? Elizabeth wondered, backing away. Amanda looked upset about something, as if she was crying, and Winston just nodded. The conversation was definitely of a personal nature. Whatever it was that they were discussing, Elizabeth had the distinct feeling that Winston wouldn't appreciate it if she came over to say hello.

Elizabeth slipped around to the back of the bleachers, unseen, and crossed the grassy field toward the station. *Something strange is going on between those two,* she thought. She could feel it deep down in the pit of her stomach. But what was it?

Elizabeth remembered the last time she had spotted the two of them together—it was at the party for the trustees. She remembered how cozy they were, sitting on the bench by

144

the pool, sipping champagne and whispering quietly to each other. Elizabeth had wanted to believe that it was a fluke—Winston was just drowning in his sorrow for Denise. But seeing them together again proved that it couldn't have been a onetime flirtation between the two of them. Even though Elizabeth was ashamed to even entertain the possibility, the question kept nagging at her: *Is Winston having an affair with the dean's wife?*

Two seconds after Winston walked in the door from his exhausting meeting with Amanda, the phone rang. He threw his jean jacket on the bed and with a loud sigh picked up the phone.

"Yeah?"

"Winston? It's Bruce."

Bruce. Just the sound of his name sent shivers of revulsion rippling on the surface of his skin. He was probably calling to gloat. *I'm Denise's boyfriend now—you're nothing.*

"What can I do for you, Bruce?" Winston asked, sounding less than friendly.

"Can you meet me and Denise at the coffeehouse in ten minutes? I want to talk to you about something important."

"I'm sure you do." Winston snorted. The meeting with Amanda had left him feeling bold and confrontational. "There's a few things I want to talk to you about too."

"Good," Bruce said in a phony voice. "I'll see you in ten?"

Winston sneered. "Maybe even sooner." He hung up the phone.

Hot blood coursed through Winston's veins. *You picked the wrong day to mess with me, Bruce.* Winston was glad they were all finally going to talk about this; he might find some sense of closure since Denise never really broke up with him to his face.

Denise and Bruce probably expected Winston to give in gracefully, to take it like a loser. *No way,* he thought, his jaw pulsating. *I'm not giving up so easily, Denise, not this time. I'm going to fight for you.* And as far as Bruce was concerned, he could take that flashy little sports car of his and drive it off the nearest cliff.

On the way to the coffeehouse Winston walked with his shoulders pulled back and his head held high, contemplating what it was going to feel like to have two black eyes and possibly a few broken ribs. The thought of being pounded to a pulp by Bruce's powerful Sigma fists didn't frighten Winston, though. What mattered was that he was finally standing up for something he believed in, instead of watching passively from the sidelines. Winston was going to take a stand.

When he reached the coffeehouse, Winston saw Denise seated in the passenger side of

146

Bruce's sleek black Porsche. She had a blinding smile and was looking cool in a pair of shades. It was amazing how quickly she'd adjusted to having a new boyfriend.

"Hop in," Denise said coyly.

"Where's Bruce?" Winston asked, glancing at the empty driver's seat. He smudged his fingerprints along the glossy black door for good measure.

"He's at Sigma house," Denise answered, giggling. "The call was just a ruse to get you out of your room." She jangled a set of silver keys in front of his face. "So, are you ready to take a spin or what?"

Winston squinted at her. "Why would I want to drive Bruce's stupid car?"

Pulling off her sunglasses, Denise stared at him with her bright blue eyes. "You're still mad at me for not going with you to the dean's party, aren't you? When are you going to get over it, Winston?" The corners of her mouth drooped. "I know how badly you've been wanting to drive this car. For weeks I've been planning with Bruce to lend you his Porsche for an evening to celebrate your new job, but you wouldn't even talk to me yesterday! What do I have to do to make you forgive me?"

Winston's mouth fell open, his eyes frozen wide with disbelief. He had been so certain that Denise had left him for Bruce, and now

147

that she telling him he was wrong, Winston wasn't quite sure what to make of it.

"That's why you've been spending so much time with Bruce?"

Denise looked at him quizzically. "What do you mean? I haven't been hanging out with him that much."

"You were in the kitchen together at the party," Winston said.

"Well, yeah, we were talking about it then—right when you walked in," Denise answered.

"What about when you two were on the library steps together?"

Denise looked confused. "When was that?"

"I saw you two when I was on the way to the dean's party," Winston said sheepishly. "I thought you were supposed to be at the beach house then."

Denise's brow furrowed. "I needed to check out a few books for bio and I happened to bump into Bruce," she said, her eyes narrowing. "What are you getting at, Winston?"

"Nothing," he said, shaking his head. The pain in his heart was subsiding and was replaced by a tranquil warmth. "I didn't think Bruce was the generous type."

"He isn't," Denise said with a laugh. "He made me do volunteer fund-raising work for the Sigmas for a whole week—that's why I've been so busy. He does have a soft spot in his heart for romance, though—but he made me swear I wouldn't tell anyone."

Winston took the corner of his shirt and rubbed away the fingerprints he had smudged on the door. "You did all that for me?" he asked.

Denise nodded. Winston's heart melted at the sight of her beautiful smile and soft curls. No one had ever gone to such lengths to surprise him before. *Denise still loves me*—the unbelievable words rang like crystal bells in his ears. Seized by a fit of passion, Winston reached through the window and cupped Denise's face in his hands. He kissed her mouth with a feverish intensity, savoring each precious moment his lips touched hers. Stroking her warm cheek, he reassured himself that this was no dream. He could feel his eyes welling up with tears as he realized that Denise was his again.

"Winnie—are you all right?" Denise asked as they parted. She looked deeply into his eyes, immediately sensing that something was bothering him. "It's the trial, isn't it?"

Winston walked over to the driver's side of the car and slid into the black leather bucket seat. "How did you find out about it?"

"Jessica told me."

"What did she say?" The gentle calm he'd been feeling was overpowered by a nervous tingling that began eating at his insides.

Denise shrugged. "Just that you identified the

149

suspect and that you were going to have to take the witness stand," she said. Brushing away a strand of hair that had fallen across his forehead, Denise tilted Winston's head toward hers and kissed him once on each cheek. "I'm really proud of you."

Just a moment before, Winston had been on top of the world, but now his euphoria crumbled, tumbling down like an avalanche. Denise had no idea what had happened with Amanda. All along he had thought that Denise was cheating on him, but it turned out that he was the only one who had been unfaithful. *If only I had known—I wouldn't be in this terrible mess,* he thought. He hated the idea of keeping it a secret from Denise, but there really was no point in telling her the truth. The little lies and deceptions had started out as innocent white snowballs rolling down a snowy hill. But now they were gathering snow with immense and uncontrollable speed, becoming so enormous that they threatened to wipe out everything in their paths.

"My testifying is not that big a deal," Winston said, looking away.

"Yes, it is! It's the bravest thing I've ever known," Denise insisted, handing him the car keys. "Now rev this baby up! We've got some serious celebrating to do!"

After Denise had dinner with Winston at his favorite pizza joint, she had him drive the

Porsche over to Sigma house, where she had organized a little get-together in his honor. Even before they exited the car, she could hear the thumping bass of the sound system and see the mass of students dancing in the living room. *This party is going to be a blast*, Denise thought proudly. *Winston really deserves to have some fun.*

"I can't go in there," Winston said before he even cut the engine. "Dinner was great, and driving the Porsche was incredible, but I'm just not in the mood to face all those people."

"Come on, Winnie," Denise pleaded, tugging at his shirtsleeve. "This party's for you. I want everyone to know what a hero my boyfriend is."

"That's just it." Winston shook his head, his grip remaining firm on the steering wheel. "I don't want you to make a big deal about this. I'm not a hero."

"Yes, you are." Denise kissed the tip of his nose. "Everyone's waiting for you. You can't let them down."

Several minutes of poking and prodding finally convinced Winston to make an appearance. Taking him by the hand, Denise led him up the steps and into Sigma house. *Once he gets into the swing of things, he'll enjoy himself,* she thought.

"Hey, everybody, Winston's here!" Denise shouted. A banner hung over the doorway that read Congratulations, Winston! People instantly flocked around the doorway, patting her boyfriend on the back and shaking his hand.

"How was the joyride?" Bruce asked with a big grin.

Winston handed him the keys. "That's one smooth car. Thanks a lot."

"No problem," Bruce answered.

Denise wrapped her arms around Winston's waist and held him close. It was nice to have him back after he had been so distant. "We brought it back with a full tank."

"And no dents," Winston added.

"It's a good thing because I'd hate to have Denise working as a permanent fund-raiser to pay off the car," Bruce said with a laugh.

"In your dreams, buddy," Denise teased.

Bruce opened a cooler filled with ice and cans of soda. "Can I offer you two something to drink?"

Denise glanced at Winston, who was still looking uneasy. "Thanks, but I think we're going to groove a little first." She took Winston by the hand and pulled him deeper into the living room. All the ugly plaid furniture the Sigmas usually had around had been moved out so that the space could be used as an impromptu dance club.

"Maybe we should leave, Denise. I'm feeling kind of tired," Winston said, standing in place.

"Don't be such a ninny, Winnie!" Denise laughed. Holding both of his hands in hers, she swung his arms back and forth in time to the hip-hop beat. "Let's get your blood pumping!"

Denise looked up to see Winston frowning. She'd never seen him looking so miserable. How could he act this way after everything she'd done for him?

"I mean it, Denise. I want to go." Winston looked dead serious.

Denise dropped Winston's hands and stopped dancing. "OK, Winnie," she said, her face falling. "We can leave if you want. Is something bothering you?"

"I just need some sleep," he said with a meek smile.

Denise wanted to believe it was a lack of sleep that was bringing him down, but she'd known Winston long enough to tell when something was truly bothering him. It was right there, in the way he looked at her. And this time Denise had a strong feeling that it was something really big.

Elizabeth cut through the crowd and spotted Winston and Denise heading for the door. While Denise glowingly entwined her arms around his, Winston looked upset about something. The scene reminded Elizabeth of the hunch she had earlier in the day, when she had spotted Winston alone with Amanda Franklin on the bleachers.

Why are they leaving so soon? Elizabeth

wondered, taking a shortcut through the kitchen. It was important she talk to him. She hadn't had a chance to thank him since the detectives told her he was going to testify on her behalf.

"Winston! Wait!" Elizabeth called, scurrying down the hallway after them.

Winston turned around and Denise smiled. "Hi, Liz," he said stiffly, as if they were only casual acquaintances. "How are you?"

Elizabeth brushed away a golden strand of hair that had escaped from her braid and smiled. "I'm much better now, thanks to you."

Winston nodded. "I guess the detectives told you."

"This afternoon," Elizabeth said. "I'm breathing a lot easier now—I don't feel the need to triple bolt my door anymore."

Denise grinned proudly and kissed Winston affectionately on the cheek. "That's my Winnie. I keep telling him he's a hero, but he doesn't believe me."

"I'm *not* a hero," Winston said emphatically. His eyes were contemplative and serious.

"See?" Denise said.

Elizabeth folded her arms and leaned against the wall. "Well, to me you are. I can't wait until we get to that trial and—"

"Sorry, Liz. We have to run," Winston said, interrupting her. He gave her a quick kiss on the cheek. "It was nice seeing you again, though."

"It was nice seeing both of you!" Elizabeth called as she watched them rush out the door.

Why did he have to leave so fast? Elizabeth wondered as the door closed behind them. Every time she saw Winston, he seemed less and less like himself. Elizabeth had the strong, undeniable suspicion that Winston was hiding something. There was a secret that he was keeping from everyone, especially Denise. And whatever the secret was that Winston was trying so desperately to protect, there was no doubt in Elizabeth's mind that Amanda Franklin was involved.

Chapter Ten

Anita Vasquez, the prosecuting attorney, approached the witness stand, carrying a legal pad filled with detailed notes. Dressed in a plum business suit, her manner was relaxed but professional. "Mr. Egbert, could you please tell the court where you were the night of the attack?" she asked with a reserved smile.

Winston swallowed a few times, his mouth as dry as cotton, and looked out over the packed courtroom. Elizabeth was sitting up front on the prosecution's side with Denise; they both nodded at him encouragingly. Amanda still hadn't showed up yet, making Winston's heart beat wildly with trepidation. *She'll show up,* soothed the voice inside his head. *Just stall for time.*

"I was in my room," Winston started slowly. He eyed the carafe of water on the attorney's desk. "May I have a glass of water?" he asked, coughing a few times for effect.

"Certainly." The attorney poured a glass and handed it to him, eating up a total of about ten seconds. Then Ms. Vasquez resumed her questioning. "What were you doing before the attack?"

"I was sleeping," Winston answered between sips of stale-tasting water.

"How long had you been asleep?"

"A half hour—maybe more," he said, stealing glances at the door. Still no Amanda.

Ms. Vasquez looked down at her notes. "And you were awakened by the sounds of a struggle coming from outside your window?"

"Objection!" called the defense attorney, James Reilly. He sat next to the suspect, who was neatly dressed in a pinstripe suit and the same black cowboy boots Winston had seen him wearing in the bar. His rattlesnake tattoo was safely covered by the long sleeves of his suit jacket. "The prosecution is leading the witness."

"Sustained," said Judge Friedman. "Please rephrase the question, Ms. Vasquez."

"Certainly, Your Honor." The attorney turned away from the judge and smiled at Winston. "Mr. Egbert, did you wake up at any time during the night?"

"Yes."

"And what was it that woke you?"

Winston folded his clammy hands in his lap. "I heard a struggle outside my window." He had repeated the story so many times that even *he* was starting to believe it was the truth. Taking a deep breath, Winston felt the tenseness in his shoulders and neck begin to melt away.

Ms. Vasquez nodded encouragingly. "And what did you do at this point?"

"I got out of bed and went to the window to see what was going on."

"And what exactly did you see?"

Winston ran his hand nervously through his neatly combed hair. It was at this point in the story when things tended to get a little mixed up. *Where are you, Amanda?* he silently demanded. She was supposed to be near the front, coaching him, but she still hadn't showed up yet. Just to be on the safe side, Winston opted for the simplest answer possible. "I saw a man dragging Elizabeth into the bushes."

Ms. Vasquez walked closer to the stand and placed her hand on the wooden partition. "The man you saw attacking Ms. Wakefield—is he in this courtroom?"

Winston nodded. "Yes."

"Would you be so kind as to point to him?"

Winston pointed to the suspect with the cowboy boots. His dark hair was slicked back, and his angular features looked just as severe as they had that day Winston saw him in the men's

159

room. He was leaning back in his chair, glaring at Winston with a stare that could melt lead.

Ms. Vasquez turned and faced the courtroom. "Let the record show, Your Honor, that Mr. Egbert pointed to the defendant, Jackson Lowe." After a few other minor questions Ms. Vasquez gave Winston a confident smile and said, "No more questions, Your Honor—the defense rests."

Just as the prosecuting attorney returned to her seat, the courtroom doors opened and Amanda strolled in. She was wearing a pink business suit and her hair fell in smooth, golden waves, making her look like a glamorous movie star from the forties. A few people turned to look as her high heels clicked up the aisle toward the front. The bailiff showed her to her seat in the third row.

It's about time, Winston thought, settling back in his seat. Their eyes locked for a long moment. *Thanks for showing up late,* he tried to communicate through his gaze. Amanda raised her eyebrows a fraction and shrugged slightly, as if to say, "Sorry—there was nothing I could do." Thankfully, Winston had made it through the first half of the hearing without any slipups. But now that Amanda had arrived, he knew he was going to make it through the second half too.

Judge Friedman pushed back his wire-rimmed spectacles and looked at the defense attorney. "Mr. Reilly, you may begin your cross-examination of the witness."

"Thank you, Your Honor." Mr. Reilly approached the witness stand without any notes, his ring-covered fingers laced behind his back.

Planting his feet solidly on the floor and holding the arms of the chair firmly, Winston braced himself for the assault. The courtroom was virtually silent except for the clean squeak of the lawyer's shoes across the marble floor. Winston saw Amanda watch him intently, ready to come to his aid with the appropriate signal or facial expression. Denise and Elizabeth sat completely still, waiting in breathless anticipation.

"Mr. Egbert, I'd like to ask you a few questions regarding what you saw on the evening in question," Mr. Reilly said, gallantly sliding his hand into the pocket of his tailored suit.

Winston blotted his sweaty palms on his dress pants.

"If you could be so kind, please describe the position of your window with respect to the scene you allegedly witnessed," the attorney said.

"My room is on the third floor," Winston began. His eyes drifted to Amanda, who was signaling him by nodding toward her right. "The attack took place to the right, in the bushes."

"In the bushes," Mr. Reilly repeated, rubbing his chin thoughtfully. "I imagine it was pretty dark in that area."

"Objection—" Ms. Vasquez stood up. "Your Honor, he's leading the witness."

"Sustained," answered the judge.

Mr. Reilly's mouth twisted into a wry smile. "Very well, Mr. Egbert, could you please explain to the court what the lighting situation was on the night of the attack?"

"It was dark, of course," Winston answered, unsure of himself. He watched as Amanda carefully mouthed the key words he was searching for. "Floodlights," he continued. "The floodlights over the building entrance lit the area."

"So you're saying, Mr. Egbert, that the lighting was sufficient for an average person to see clearly from a third-floor window."

"That's correct," Winston answered.

Mr. Reilly pursed his lips and began pacing back and forth in front of the witness stand. It was taking him so long to come up with a second question that Winston was starting to think he'd stumped him. "Mr. Egbert," the attorney finally said, "please tell the court what you do before going to bed every night—what is your regular routine?"

He's digging for questions, Winston thought with silent satisfaction. *The defense has no case at all.* Inhaling deeply, Winston felt his body relax. He took his time, enjoying his moment in the spotlight.

"I like to read a little or watch some TV, then I change into my pajamas, take out my contacts, brush my teeth—"

"Did you follow this same procedure the night of the attack?"

"Yes," Winston answered.

Mr. Reilly nodded. "Then you went to sleep?"

"Yes—I was woken up about a half hour later by the sound outside my window." Winston made eye contact with the judge.

"That's when you went to the window and saw the attack?" Mr. Reilly asked.

Winston looked back at the defense attorney. "That's correct."

"You did nothing else in between? You just woke up and ran to the window?"

"Yes!" Winston said abruptly. *Why doesn't the judge wrap this up?* he wondered. Each question was more insipid than the last.

But Mr. Reilly grinned smugly, as if he thought his line of questioning was clever. Folding his arms across his chest with satisfaction, he stared Winston down. "Mr. Egbert, how well do you see without your contacts?"

Winston's confidence suddenly shriveled like a leaky balloon. "I can see pretty well," he lied.

"Are you nearsighted or farsighted?"

"Farsighted," Winston lied again. Looking into the crowd, he saw Amanda biting her lower lip nervously. Winston didn't dare look at Denise or Elizabeth.

Mr. Reilly stopped pacing. "So we are to assume that even without your contacts, you were able to clearly identify the defendant, Mr. Jackson Lowe, as the attacker?"

"Yes," Winston answered softly.

"Forgive me, Mr. Egbert, if I'm not comfortable making assumptions," the attorney said. Turning to the judge, he said, "I'd like to ask the court's permission to have Mr. Egbert take his contacts out so that we may be more certain of what he did and did not see on the evening of the attack."

"Your Honor, I object!" shouted Ms. Vasquez.

"Overruled," the judge answered. "You may proceed, Mr. Reilly."

I am in deep trouble. Winston's stomach suddenly felt as if it were doing a free fall off the edge of the Grand Canyon. *Now they'll know I'm a fraud.* Amanda's eyes were wide, and she started doing subtle but frantic hand gestures, trying to convey a message to him. As if she were playing a game of charades, Amanda pretended to be taking out a contact lens, then put the imaginary lens in her cupped hand. Turning her cupped hand upside down, she bent over, apparently looking for it.

"If you would be so kind, Mr. Egbert, could you please remove your lenses for the court?" the attorney asked.

Instantly the message clicked in Winston's brain. "Excuse me, Your Honor, but if I take out my lenses, I'll have nowhere to put them—they'll be ruined."

"You don't have a lens case with you?" the judge asked.

"No," Winston answered. *This is the out I've been looking for. Thank you, Amanda.*

Mr. Reilly walked over to where the defendant was sitting and opened his briefcase. "That won't be a problem, Your Honor. I have my own case with me, which Mr. Egbert may use."

The tiny hairs on the back of Winston's neck stood straight on end as the lawyer handed him the case. He took one last, clear look at Amanda who was mouthing the words, "Watch me," then took out his lenses.

"How are we doing?" Mr. Reilly asked when he was finished.

"Fine," Winston answered, trying to rub away the white haze that covered his eyes.

"Can you see me?"

"Yes," Winston answered, following the soft, fuzzy shape of Mr. Reilly as he started walking away from the witness stand.

"Good. Now we're going to test your sight a little bit." With that, the defense attorney walked down the center aisle, his figure fading into the blurry mass of the courtroom. Judging from the sound of his steps, Winston estimated that Mr. Reilly had walked all the way to the back of the room.

"The point at which I'm standing is probably one-third the distance of where the attacker was." Mr. Reilly's voice echoed through the room. "Can you still see me, Mr. Egbert?"

"Yes," Winston lied for a third time.

"All right, then. I'm going to raise my hand, and you tell me how many fingers I'm holding up."

The bleary fog in front of Winston's eyes turned the courtroom into an unrecognizable patchwork of muted colors. One color blended into the next, making the defense attorney indistinguishable from the heavy wooden doors at the back. Winston's unfocused eyes panned the hazy tapestry, coming to rest on a bright pink blotch in the third row. *Thank goodness Amanda wore pink,* Winston thought.

"How many fingers do you see?" Mr. Reilly repeated.

Winston looked at the pink blotch for the answer. Light was flickering around her, as if she was moving her arms or something to signal him. She might even have been mouthing the words, but Winston would have never known. His eyesight was so poor that if he hadn't known it was Amanda in the pink suit, he might have assumed that there was an overgrown ball of cotton candy sitting in the third row.

I'm doomed, Winston thought, feeling sweat bead across his forehead. *There's no way out of this one.*

The judge turned to Winston, his wrinkled mouth puckering impatiently. "Mr. Egbert— we're *waiting*."

What in the world is going on here? Elizabeth was sitting on the edge of the bench, watching Winston sweating on the witness stand. He squinted to the point where his eyes nearly disappeared in his head—it was obvious that he was having trouble seeing. *I just don't get it,* she thought. *How could Winston see the attacker three stories down, in the dark, if he can hardly see across the room in broad daylight?*

Denise clutched Elizabeth's arm. "I can't take this," she whispered, her voice wavering. "They're making a fool out of him."

"Is it that hard for him to see?" Elizabeth whispered back.

Denise nodded. "Winnie's as blind as a bat without his contacts."

"Maybe he left them in by mistake."

"I doubt it," Denise answered. Her blue eyes were shadowed with worry. "He's really careful about that sort of thing."

Elizabeth looked across the room to the

167

defense's side, where Jackson Lowe was sitting. He was slumped down in his chair, long legs stretched out in front of him, his cowboy boots crossed at the ankles. She looked in morbid fascination at his strong, thick hands, the ones that had nearly taken her life. Jackson's thin lips were smiling, laughing at Winston, openly enjoying the scene that was taking place. Already he seemed to know that he was going to be a free man.

Elizabeth looked away, disgusted by Jackson's self-satisfied smirk and nonchalant attitude. *We can't let this guy go free.* She leaned toward Denise. "Isn't there a chance Winston put on his glasses before he looked out the window?"

"His glasses are broken," Denise whispered.

Mr. Reilly was still holding his arm up, with three fingers in the air. "Once again, Mr. Egbert, how many fingers am I holding up?"

"Two?" Winston guessed.

Mr. Reilly shook his head and smiled, apparently pleased with the answer. "Let me give you another chance," he said, holding up four fingers this time. "How about now?"

Elizabeth looked away again. The tension in the courtroom was like a massive weight pressing down on them. While Winston contemplated his second guess, undoubtedly hoping to be luckier this time, Elizabeth scanned the crowd. The hard wooden bench seats were generally filled with executive types, a few school officials, and some local townspeople. Looking over her shoulder, she spotted Amanda Franklin in a pink business suit.

What is she doing here? Elizabeth wondered silently. Everyone else probably thought Amanda was there to represent her husband, but Elizabeth knew better. The tingling sensation in the pit of Elizabeth's stomach once again told her that Amanda's connection to Winston went much deeper than merely being his boss's wife.

"Mr. Egbert—your answer, please," Mr. Reilly called from the back of the courtroom.

Elizabeth stole another glance over her shoulder, pretending to look at the attorney but all the while watching Amanda. At the moment Amanda's brow was wrinkled, her face taut with concentration. *Did I just see her mouth the answer to Winston?* Elizabeth looked again. Amanda's lips were silently moving, all right, slowly and carefully saying the word *four*. As a backup she carefully raised four fingers and rested them on the lapel of her jacket. There was no doubt about it—she was giving Winston the answers.

Denise leaned against Elizabeth's arm and closed her eyes. "I can't watch this," she whispered. "Just tell me when it's over."

Elizabeth nodded and looked up at Winston, who was squinting in Amanda's direction. That was where he had been looking during most of the hearing. Was Amanda giving him the answers then too? Suddenly the missing piece of the puzzle locked into place. Elizabeth understood everything.

I hate to break it to you, Denise, Elizabeth thought sadly. *But this is far from over.*

"One?" Winston answered, his confident voice now just a murmur.

The courtroom erupted into a wave of whispers and comments. Jackson Lowe leaned back comfortably in his chair while he watched the poor, sad sack on the witness stand make a total idiot of himself. *What's this guy trying to prove anyway?* He wasn't the one who was in the window that night. *Why is he testifying?* Thanks to this guy, Jackson was going to get away with it. *I have to remember to thank this loser personally when the trial is over.*

Jackson patted the pocket of the itchy business suit the lawyer made him rent and thought about the fresh pack of smokes he was going to break into when he got outside. *A whiskey wouldn't be too bad either.* Before the trial Jackson had told himself that if he got off without any jail time, he'd just hop into his truck and keep driving north until he found another sleepy little town. But now he was starting to think it would be better to stick around. Now that he was no longer a suspect, he could get away with murder—*so to speak,* he thought with a laugh.

"I'm going to give you one last try, Mr. Egbert," the lawyer said. "How many fingers am I holding up now?"

The puny guy cowered in his chair, his face drenched in sweat. *Come on, you runt, give him an answer so I can get out of here.* For some reason Mr. Egbert wasn't looking at the lawyer; his eyes were focused on the crowd. Jackson exhaled impatiently, his own eyes following the runt's gaze.

That was when he spotted her.

She was wearing pink. He probably wouldn't have recognized her if it hadn't been for her hair. It was golden, silky blond with big curls. Jackson remembered standing in the hedges, looking up at the third-floor window, seeing that woman looking down at him, her blond curls tumbling out the window. *She* was the real witness.

"Four?" Winston answered. Someone in the back of the courtroom snickered. The attorney walked to the front of the room, still holding two fingers in the air, and walked all the way to the witness stand.

You're a good man, Mr. Reilly.

The lawyer thrust his hand right under Winston's nose. "How many fingers?"

"Two," the little weasel answered. He looked like he was about to break down and cry like a baby.

"And I can assume, Mr. Egbert," the lawyer continued triumphantly, "that you don't have a pair of eyeglasses?"

"They're broken," the sniveling creep answered quietly, shaking his head in defeat.

Let's get the show on the road, Jackson thought eagerly, turning his attention back to the blond in pink. His thirst for whiskey suddenly disappeared. There were more important things to take care of first.

I hope you're ready, pretty lady, Jackson thought, puckering his lips in her direction. *Because I'm coming after you.*

Chapter
Eleven

"Order in the court!" Judge Friedman banged his gavel to quell the sudden commotion that had rippled through the courtroom. The district attorney tossed her pen on the desk in surrender, shaking her head. Denise and Elizabeth shared the same expression of wide-eyed disbelief. In the midst of the courtroom uproar Amanda stood up and quietly slipped out the door.

Winston hung his head in defeat and shame. He didn't dare look at Jackson's face, but he didn't need to—he could feel the killer's triumphant grin beaming in his direction.

Mr. Reilly resumed his pacing as Winston popped his lenses back in. "Your Honor, if Mr. Egbert is unable to see clearly at such a short distance in bright light, I find it virtually impossible that he would be able to identify my client at three

173

times the distance in the dark of night," the attorney said. "Perhaps Mr. Egbert was sleepwalking."

"Clearly Mr. Egbert is not a credible witness," the judge replied, banging the gavel again. "This case is dismissed. Mr. Lowe, you are free to go."

The killer shook hands with Mr. Reilly while Winston stepped down from the witness stand. Ms. Vasquez's mouth remained pinched in a sour expression as Winston approached her; she didn't say a word to him. Winston's body felt sluggish and heavy as he walked past Ms. Vasquez and over to where Denise and Elizabeth waited for him. They both looked sad and disappointed, yet they still seemed supportive at the same time. Their loyalty broke Winston's heart.

"I'm sorry," he muttered, his voice cracking. "I let you down, Elizabeth."

Elizabeth's brow creased as she watched Jackson Lowe walk out of the courtroom. "You did the best you could," she said.

Denise wrapped her arms around Winston and kissed his cheek. "Don't feel bad, Winnie. You were only trying to do what was right."

Throughout the whole mess Winston had told himself over and over again that he'd only been trying to do what was right, but now he wasn't so sure he believed it anymore. All the best intentions in the world weren't enough to bring the killer to justice.

Detectives Reese and Martin walked up to Winston. "Can we speak with you for a moment, Mr. Egbert?" Martin asked.

Denise kissed Winston on the cheek again. "We'll be waiting for you in the car," she whispered in his ear.

Staring down at his feet, Winston tried to ignore the sharp acid that was churning in his stomach. The detectives closed in around him like hungry vultures waiting for their next meal.

"Why didn't you tell us you wore contacts?" Detective Martin asked.

Winston shrugged, still not daring to look at them. "It never came up—I forgot about it."

"You forgot about it?" Martin repeated, his voice taking on an edge. "How could you *forget* to mention something so important? Do you realize how much time and money and energy you've wasted because you *forgot* to tell us about this small detail?"

"Not to mention the harassment of an innocent man," Reese added.

Martin pointed at Winston, the tip of his finger jabbing into Winston's chest. "You're lucky the judge didn't charge you with perjury," he said in a low voice. With that, Detective Martin walked away.

Reese hung behind for a moment, hovering over Winston threateningly. "What else have you lied about, Winston?" he growled. "If I were you, I'd keep my nose clean—because if you make one wrong move, I'll be waiting for you."

"Winston, open up! It's Liz." Elizabeth knocked on the door for a third time. Winston was slow to answer, but Elizabeth knew he was in his room because she could hear rustling coming from the other side of the door. She'd already given him a few hours to recover from the trauma of the trial, but too many questions were scorching inside her. And she wasn't about to leave until she got some answers.

After a few minutes Winston finally opened the door. He was dressed in a pair of dirty sweats, and his eyes were sunken and dark, taking some of the bite out of Elizabeth's anger. "What is it, Liz?" he asked mournfully.

Elizabeth walked into his room and closed the door behind her. "I need to talk to you," she said, smoothing out the bitterness in her voice. "Is Denise here?"

"No," he answered, dropping weakly into a chair. "Have a seat."

Elizabeth sat down. She had been rehearsing what she was going to say for hours, but suddenly the words caught in her throat. "I have some questions that need answering," she began.

Winston grabbed a brown corduroy throw pillow that was lying on the floor and hugged it to his chest. "I know you have a lot on your mind, but can this wait until tomorrow? I'm really fried."

"No, this can't wait!" Elizabeth snapped, throwing her hands up in the air. "A killer went free today, and I want to know why you, who supposedly witnessed the attack, couldn't put him away!"

Winston swallowed hard. "The lawyer was a sly one," he said ruefully. "You saw the way he tricked me."

Elizabeth shook her head. "That was no trick, Winston. That was a legitimate test."

He bowed his head, pressing his cheek against the pillow. "Maybe I just imagined what he looked like—you know, sometimes the mind can fill in details for you."

"We both know that Jackson Lowe is the killer," Elizabeth countered. "Something obviously led you to him."

Winston shook his head and didn't say anything.

Elizabeth had a sudden, desperate urge to take Winston by the shoulders and shake enough sense into him to get him to come clean. She threw a verbal punch instead. "I know Amanda Franklin is involved."

Winston looked up at her, chaos flickering behind his eyes. "Who—"

"I've seen you two together quite a bit. I even saw her today in the courtroom,"

Elizabeth said, laying all the cards out on the table. "She's a beautiful, persuasive woman, Winston. And I have a sneaking suspicion that you two have gotten quite close recently."

Winston choked back tears, looking both frightened and relieved at the same time. "Please don't tell Denise—it was a stupid mistake."

Unwavered by Winston's emotional outburst, Elizabeth folded her arms across her chest, promising nothing. "What happened, Winston? Tell me everything. I have a right to know."

Winston sighed deeply, clutching the corners of the pillow for dear life. "It was the night of the dean's party. She was flirting with me right out in the open. I was kind of nervous about it, but excited too. After a while she asked me to meet her in the garden—but I didn't. I ran out of there as quickly as I could. That's when I met up with you outside."

"And then?"

"I came back here." Winston wiped his wet eyes with the sleeve of his sweatshirt. "I was getting ready for bed when I heard a knock at the door. It was Amanda."

Elizabeth sat down. "You let her in?"

"She kind of let herself in." He paused. "OK, I'll admit it—I was incredibly attracted to her."

Elizabeth nodded unsympathetically. "While this was going on, did it ever occur to you that you had made a commitment to Denise?"

"See, that's the thing," Winston said defensively. "At the time I thought Denise was cheating on me with Bruce Patman. I thought it was over between us. You know, you saw them together on the steps of the library."

Elizabeth had to admit to herself that even she thought Denise and Bruce had looked a little suspicious that evening. "Did you even once stop to think about your boss?"

Winston looked down at the pillow. "Actually, I did. That's why I stopped Amanda from taking it as far as she wanted to go. I suddenly decided that it was a huge mistake and was about to ask her to leave when she looked out the window and saw the attack."

"She called you over to the window, but you couldn't see anything because your contacts were already out by then," Elizabeth added.

"Exactly," Winston said, his eyes meeting hers. "You know, Liz—I wanted to report it right away, but Amanda's the one who stopped me. She was afraid that if we called the cops, everyone would find out that we'd been together. You see my dilemma, don't you?"

Elizabeth's face grew hot. "I see your dilemma, Winston, but it's still no excuse. That guy almost killed me! You've made one bad decision after another, and people are dying because of it!"

Winston cringed. "I didn't mean to hurt anyone!"

"I don't care what your intentions were; you have to take responsibility for what you've done!" Elizabeth was seething, her eyes glowing fiercely. "Next time this guy strikes, the victim could be Denise," she shouted, heading for the door. "And she might not be as lucky as I was!"

Tuesday morning, when Winston arrived at work, the door to the dean's office was closed. He felt terrible about lying to the dean yesterday, when he called in sick in order to go to the assault hearing. But there was nothing else he could do. Debating whether or not to knock on the door and tell his boss he was there, Winston decided to just sit down at his own desk and start working. He needed the mindlessness of paperwork to take his thoughts off his grim future.

Winston poured himself a cup of black coffee and took a sip. For days his brain had throbbed from worry, juggling truth and lies, and staging elaborate deceptions. For once he didn't want to think about anything. He wanted his mind to be totally blank.

The door to the dean's office opened slowly, and Dean Franklin came out, his features creased unmistakably with distress. "Good morning, Winston," he said in a low voice. "There are some men here to see you."

"Huh?" Winston nearly choked on his coffee as the door opened wider and Detectives

Martin and Reese walked out. The room started spinning, and Winston grabbed the edge of his desk to steady himself.

"We'd like you to come down to the station to answer a few questions, Mr. Egbert," Martin said, shoving his hands into the pockets of his gray overcoat.

"But I—I already answered your questions," Winston stuttered, his eyes darting wildly from the dean to the detectives. Did the dean know what was going on?

Reese regarded Winston with a piercing stare. "These are different questions."

Dean Franklin's mouth took on a harsh line. "Gentlemen, would it be all right if I had a moment to speak with Winston alone?"

"Certainly," Martin answered, heading for the door. "We'll be waiting outside."

"We'll give him a chance to finish his coffee," Reese said, looking snidely at Winston's cup. "Did you just suddenly pick up a caffeine habit, Winston?"

Winston's heart felt as if it were going to burst right out of his chest. For a brief moment, as he watched the detectives leave, he contemplated jumping out the office window and taking off for Mexico.

"Son, is there something you'd like to talk about?" Dean Franklin asked, leaning against Winston's desk.

"Not really," Winston mumbled. Humiliation burned on his cheeks. "What did they say to you?"

"They asked me a few questions about you—about your character," the dean said, rubbing his forehead. "I told them that you seemed to be a hardworking, responsible, conscientious individual, but to be honest, I hadn't known you long enough to really vouch for you."

Winston nodded slowly. "I understand."

"Are you in some kind of trouble?"

Nothing I can tell you about, Winston thought sadly. Once again Dean Franklin was showing Winston much more kindness than he deserved. Winston wanted so badly to confide in him. He must have been completely out of his mind to ever betray the man's trust.

"It's not as serious as you may think," Winston said. "But I have to take care of it myself."

Dean Franklin stared at him for several minutes, not saying anything. "I take it your parents don't know."

Winston shook his head. "I'd rather not have them find out."

The dean nodded understandingly. Taking a gold pen out of his shirt pocket, he jotted down two numbers and an address. "Amanda and I are going to the theater tonight, but if you need me for anything at all, please call my beeper. We should be home after eleven if you want to call me then."

Winston took the card. "You have no idea how much I appreciate this, sir."

"I just hope you can straighten out this mess, whatever it is."

"Me too," Winston answered, moving toward the door. With a feeling of doom in his chest, Winston walked out of the office to join the two detectives who were waiting for him.

Denise walked up the paved walkway leading to the administration building, her green backpack slung over one shoulder. Walking into the main entrance of the building, Denise signed in at the front desk, writing *Dean Franklin's office* as her destination.

It was a spur-of-the-moment decision—she happened to be walking by the building—but a deep tugging from her heart told her to drop by and say hi to Winston. After bombing on the witness stand, he had become even more withdrawn. Even though the hearing was over, she was sure something inside Winston just wouldn't let him put the situation to rest.

And I'm afraid to ask what it is, Denise thought wearily as she walked past the registrar's office and continued toward the elevator at the end of the hallway. There were too many things that didn't make sense about Winston's testimony. But Denise trusted Winston wholeheartedly. If he wasn't telling her something, it was because the time wasn't right. When Winston was ready, he'd fill her in on the rest.

Denise looked at the panel above the elevator, watching the numbers light up one at a time in descending order as the car came down. When the number one lit up, Denise stepped forward. The elevator doors opened.

"Winston?" Denise gasped aloud when she saw her boyfriend coming out of the car, escorted by the two detectives she had seen at the trial.

"Denise?" Winston stood next to her, the detectives following closely as if he were a criminal. "Why are you here?"

Denise had the strange sensation that she was in the wrong place at the wrong time—it was kind of like showing up at your own surprise party an hour early. "I was coming by to say hi," she said, staring at the detectives' dour faces. "Winston, what's going on?"

Winston shook off the detectives. "Do you mind?" he said, glaring at them. They took only half a step back. "They're bringing me in for questioning."

"Again? What is this all about?"

"I'm not sure," he answered. Judging from the look of panic in Winston's deep brown eyes, Denise knew he was telling the truth. "But there's nothing to be alarmed about. They're probably just going to ask me a few routine questions."

Denise's blood ran cold. One look at the detectives' hard faces told her this was no routine interview. "I'm going with you," she said with determination.

"No—please don't."

"Winnie, you can't go through this alone," Denise insisted. "Let me be there for you."

Martin stepped forward and clamped his hand firmly on Winston's shoulder. "We should get going. They're expecting us."

"Winnie—"

"It's all right," Winston said, touching her hand. His fingers were damp and cold. "I'll come over and see you later, OK?" He kissed her tenderly on the lips.

Denise's throat felt tight, as if it were closing in on her. "Promise me you'll be all right."

Winston turned with the detectives as they started walking down the stark corridor. "Just remember that I love you," he said weakly as they took him away.

Instead of being questioned in Detective Martin's office, Winston was led all the way down the long hallway, beyond the holding cells, to the interrogation room. There was nothing on the gray walls, and the windows were barred. In the center of the room a table and four chairs were bolted to the floor.

"Would you like some coffee?" Reese

asked, waving a Styrofoam cup in front of Winston. Before he had a chance to refuse, the detective said, "Oh, I forgot—caffeine makes you edgy? Or doesn't it? I can't seem to keep your stories straight."

Winston ignored Reese, staring at the blank gray wall to the right of Detective Martin. It still wasn't clear to him why they brought him back, but every nerve-racking moment spent in the drab interrogation room told him that it couldn't be good.

"Let me get straight to the point, Egbert," Detective Martin said. The formality and graciousness he had shown during previous questioning sessions had totally disappeared. "Now that Mr. Lowe has been crossed off our suspect list, we've been doing a little digging around for evidence. Yesterday Detective Reese and I went to Gangbusters and spoke with a few people there, and they had some interesting things to tell us."

Winston starting breathing heavily. "Jackson Lowe was there that night; anyone there could tell you that."

Reese placed his palms flat on the table and leaned toward Winston. "The funny thing is, *Egbert,* no one seemed to remember seeing Jackson at the bar—but they all seem to remember seeing *you.*"

Martin pulled out a notepad from his shirt pocket and read from it. "A waitress named

Rachel claims you tried to order an alcoholic beverage without correct identification, refused to pay for the soda she gave you, created a disturbance, refused to leave when asked . . ." He flipped over the page with an angry flourish and continued. "Picked a fight with four customers, and were finally thrown out by a bartender named Walter."

Winston laughed nervously. "That's blown way out of proportion."

"Nearly everyone in the bar that night was able to corroborate the waitress's story," Reese added in a menacing tone.

"What are you getting at?" Winston shouted. Anxiety ran up his spine like hot needles.

Martin twisted his lips thoughtfully. "Someone spotted you sitting in your car in the parking lot behind Gangbusters for nearly an hour. What were you doing there?"

A raw, fiery ball of tension caught in Winston's throat. "I was just sitting there, waiting."

"Waiting for what?" Reese snapped, leaning closer.

"I don't know."

"Were you alone?" Martin asked.

Winston paused. "Yes."

Both detectives fell silent and made eye contact with each other. Finally Martin spoke. "Why did you attack Elizabeth Wakefield?"

Winston's eyes bulged. "I didn't attack her! Why would I attack my friend?"

187

"That's what we want to know," Reese said, bearing down on him.

Martin referred to his notebook again. "She was walking near your building late at night. Maybe you were waiting to pounce on someone else instead. Maybe you attacked Elizabeth by accident."

Winston's mouth went dry. The back of his striped rugby shirt was damp with sweat. "I would never hurt anyone," he said solemnly. "Elizabeth said that the guy who attacked her had a southern accent. Doesn't Jackson Lowe have a southern accent?"

Reese sneered at Winston. "Maybe you were just trying to throw her off your trail," he said. "Personally, I don't think you're smart enough to think of something as clever as that."

Martin leaned back in his chair. "You haven't been straight with us, Winston. Your story about witnessing the attack from your room just doesn't fly. You're hiding something, aren't you?"

Winston said nothing, feeling the heat rise up from underneath his collar. All he had to do was say Amanda's name—tell them the whole story—and they'd understand and let him off the hook. But the words caught in Winston's throat. It had nothing to do with Amanda. He felt no particular loyalty to her so much as he felt he needed to protect Dean Franklin and Denise. If the story got out, it could destroy them both.

"What do you have to say for yourself, Killer?" Reese flashed Winston an antagonistic smile.

Winston folded his arms stubbornly across his chest. "Nothing," he said. "You have no evidence linking me to either crime."

"Is that a fact?" Martin said, sharing a hearty laugh with Detective Reese. "Well, let me tell you something, Egbert. Your whereabouts on the nights of both murders have not been accounted for. Unless you come up with a decent alibi, you just might be spending the rest of your life in prison."

"Do you have anything to say for yourself now?" Reese asked.

Winston cradled his head in his shaking hands. "I want to see a lawyer."

Chapter
Twelve

Denise came crashing through the door of the WSVU station as if she were about to announce that the world was going to end. Her face, frightened and confused, was streaked with tears and her chest heaved with shallow breaths. But it was the terrible, lost look in her eyes that made Elizabeth drop the videotapes she was carrying and run to Denise's side.

"What happened?" Elizabeth asked, leading Denise to a chair. Luckily everyone had left for lunch, so they had some privacy. Elizabeth handed Denise a tissue from a nearby box. "Are you all right?"

Denise shook her head. "The detectives came and took Winston away," she gasped between sobs. "And I don't know why."

Elizabeth sank into the chair next to her. Apparently the detectives also had a hunch that there was more to the story than Winston was willing to admit. She hoped that this time he'd at least have the sense to tell the truth.

"What did he say?" Elizabeth asked, placing a consoling arm on Denise's shoulder. She felt bad for Denise—being so innocently entangled in the disaster her boyfriend had gotten himself into. The worst part was, Denise had no idea what was actually going on.

"All he said was that I should remember that he loved me." Denise broke down, resting her head on her arms. "What did he mean by that? Are they going to send him to prison? What did he do?"

Elizabeth didn't have an answer to any of those questions. "I'm sure everything is going to be fine, Denise. You just have to trust that it will all work out."

Denise lifted her head, tears staining her face. "You know something, don't you?"

"What do you mean?" Elizabeth shifted uncomfortably in her chair. She didn't like the position she was suddenly finding herself in. She didn't want to lie to Denise, but she also didn't think it was her place to tell her about what her boyfriend had done.

"I mean, you know more about this than I do—don't you?" Denise dried her tear-stained cheeks. "There's something he's not telling me."

Elizabeth fell silent, knowing that regardless

192

of whether she told Denise yes or no, the answer would weigh heavily on her conscience.

"It's all right, Liz. Whatever it is, I can handle it." Denise dried her eyes. "Just don't keep the truth from me."

Elizabeth exhaled, feeling torn between her loyalty to Winston and her sense of fairness toward Denise. Still, she couldn't justify lying to Denise, especially since her future was so entwined with Winston's. She had a right to know.

"You're right—there is more to the story," Elizabeth started slowly. "I found out about it myself only yesterday."

Denise looked up, her eyes full of hope of at last unlocking the mystery. Elizabeth felt a pang of misery in her heart, understanding how badly Denise wanted to know the truth and at the same time being fully aware of how much it was going to hurt. "Let me start out by saying that Winston feels miserable about what happened—he knows what an enormous mistake he's made."

"What mistake?" Denise cried.

Elizabeth reluctantly continued. "He loves you very much, you know."

"Liz—you're scaring me," Denise said, her face turning pale. "Please get to it."

Gripping the edge of the table, Elizabeth readied herself for the tidal wave of emotion that was about to hit. "Winston wasn't the one who witnessed the attack—someone else did."

Denise's eyes clouded uncomprehendingly. "Who?"

Elizabeth chewed her lower lip. "The person who was with him that night."

Struggling to catch her breath, Denise pressed on bravely. "Liz—who was with him that night?"

Please forgive me, Winston—this is something I have to do. Elizabeth drew in a deep breath before saying the earth-shattering words. "Amanda Franklin—the dean's wife."

Clasping her hand over her mouth, Denise muted the horrible cry of surprise that escaped her throat. Fresh tears welled up in her anguished eyes.

"He admits it was a huge mistake," Elizabeth said quickly, trying to soften the blow. "And that he stopped her before it went too far. He said he did it because he thought you were leaving him for Bruce."

Denise's distraught expression hardened into ice. "How dare he blame me!" she shouted. "What on earth gave him that idea?"

Elizabeth suddenly found herself defending someone she herself was disgusted with. "There were some rumors circulating about you and Bruce."

"Don't waste your breath defending that lech," Denise shouted, getting to her feet.

"I've heard enough!" She stormed out of the room, slamming the door behind her.

Either it was intuition, or maybe it was because she knew him so well, but somehow Denise sensed that Winston would be beating down her door later that afternoon, ready to confess. That was why she spent a few hours composing herself, preparing for a confrontation. When Winston finally did arrive at her dorm room, Denise opened the door, cool as a cucumber, ready to let him have it.

"Hi—I'm so glad you're home," Winston said, coming into her room. He tried to kiss her, but Denise turned her lips away from him, giving her cheek instead.

"What happened at the police station?" she asked flatly, hands on hips.

Winston took off his jean jacket and tossed it on Denise's bed. "It was a nightmare—but I don't want to get into it right now," he said seriously. "There's something I need to talk to you about."

Denise opened her eyes wide, feigning innocence. "What is it, Winnie? What's wrong?"

"I haven't been completely honest with you," Winston began, sitting down on her futon.

Completely honest. The phrase left a bitter aftertaste in Denise's mouth. *Totally dishonest is more like it.*

195

"There's something about the whole trial I didn't tell you." Winston paused, his face turning various shades of red.

It would have been so easy for Denise to let him off the hook—to tell him she already knew the whole story and save him the pain of confessing to her. But her wounds were still fresh, and Denise couldn't resist making him squirm.

Denise folded her arms in front of her. "Why do you look so upset, Winnie? You can tell me—it can't be that bad."

"It's pretty bad, Denise," he said tiredly. "I'm so afraid you're going to hate me."

"Don't be silly, Winnie," Denise cooed, sitting on his lap. "The only thing you could possibly do that would make me hate you is cheat on me."

Winston swallowed audibly. Now that Denise had successfully backed him into a corner, primed for the kill, she realized that her heart was no longer in it. She loved Winston, despite what he had done, and she just couldn't hurt him back.

"Spit it out, Winston," Denise said impatiently.

Winston's jaw fell open and he sat there, motionless, as if his brain were frozen.

Denise stood up, her fake smile fading. "Let me help you out—you cheated on me with the dean's wife," she said as matter-of-factly as humanly possible. She brushed her hands together. "There—that was easy."

"Who told you?" Winston smacked his fist into his open palm. He didn't look at her.

Denise angrily kicked aside a pair of jeans she had left in the corner. Pacing the room, she looked for other objects to take her fury out on. "It was Elizabeth—I made her tell me. I deserved to know, Winston."

"You're right," he whispered, his voice cracking. "I just didn't know how to tell you. This happened when I thought you were seeing Bruce."

Running both hands through her thick curls, Denise let out a frustrated grunt. "That's what Elizabeth told me, and you know what? I think it's a pretty lame excuse. If you thought there was something going on, you should've confronted me directly instead of going behind my back with that—that bimbo!"

Winston moaned, covering his face with his hands. "It wasn't worth it at all. I knew the whole time that I was making a huge mistake. I couldn't stop thinking about you—"

"Don't give me that!" Denise screamed, her blood reaching the boiling point. "The only person you thought about was yourself, Winston Egbert!"

Tears rolled down Winston's face, splitting Denise's heart in two. "Denise, please, how many times can I say I'm sorry? I'm in serious trouble right now, and I need your help."

"Get out!" Denise screamed.

Winston touched her arm and she pulled away. "Denise . . . please just listen to me for a minute."

"I said get out! I don't want to hear your excuses!" Denise opened the door, praying he would leave before she burst into tears. "I never want to see you again!"

Winston crouched down in the bushes in front of the dean's house, knowing full well that it was a risky venture—but he had no other choice. Somehow it always came back to Amanda, and now that she was his only alibi, Winston needed her more than ever.

Dusk was falling. Time was passing too quickly and nothing was happening to prove his innocence. Already Winston had numbed himself, accepting prison as the inevitable conclusion to the nightmare that had become his life.

Staring at the empty driveway, Winston thought about Denise. The fury that smoldered in her eyes was enough to make Winston's heart stop beating altogether. He never thought he'd be able to incite such anger in her. *But I deserve it,* he thought. *Now I've lost her for good.* Now that Denise didn't want to see him anymore, there was very little left for him to live for.

A few moments later a sleek black Jaguar turned into the long driveway. The garage door opened automatically, and Winston's weary eyes followed the car and driver as they rolled into the parking space. The driver was Amanda. And she was alone.

As soon as he heard the engine shut off, Winston came out of the bushes and walked to the garage. Amanda was just getting out of the car, her arms loaded down with shopping bags. While he was spending most of his day at the police station, she was at the mall.

"Do you need some help with that?" he asked.

Amanda whirled around, nearly dropping her merchandise. "Winston! You scared me!" She stared at him, her eyes narrowing. "What are you doing here?"

Winston didn't bother with pleasantries—he cut right to the chase. "The police are after me, Amanda. They think I'm the murderer."

Amanda's arms dropped to her sides, spilling the bags onto the floor. "How on earth is that possible?"

"It's complicated," Winston said numbly. "I'm not going to go into the details. The point is I need an alibi for the night of the attack and the night I followed Jackson Lowe to Gangbusters."

"So?"

"So if I don't get one, they're going to charge me with murder," he answered, clenching his jaw. "I need you to clear my name."

Amanda bent down and started picking up the ripped shopping bags. "You never should've come here—someone might see you."

"You know what, Amanda? I don't really care anymore," Winston answered through bared teeth. The veins in his neck pulsed. "My life is on the line here. It's about time we put it all out in the open."

"No way," Amanda said fiercely. "I have too much to protect."

"And I don't?" Winston shouted. He looked with disgust at the shopping bags filled with new clothes and shoes. "I hope you can still enjoy your little shopping sprees while I'm rotting away in a prison cell!"

"Let me tell you something, Winston. I'm *sick* of this harassment," Amanda seethed. "You call me on the phone all the time, begging to meet with you in different places—"

"I only called when I absolutely had to."

"And now you start showing up at my home, demanding things from me. You have no right to bother me like this!" Amanda's lips quivered in anger.

Winston slammed his fist down on the hood of Amanda's car, making her jump. "You are the most selfish, conniving person I have ever met!"

Amanda put the bags on the floor again and took out a cellular phone from her purse.

"Go ahead and call the cops," Winston

shouted, shaking his head in disbelief. "I'm already on my way to jail as it is."

"I'm not going to call the cops," Amanda said coolly. She wielded the phone like a weapon, confident it was going to help her take control of the situation. "You either get off my property right this second or I make two phone calls—the first one, to your girlfriend."

"She already knows," Winston said boldly. "Who else?"

An evil smile twisted Amanda's pale mouth as she began dialing a number. "I'm calling my husband. I want to tell him about how you've been stalking me."

Chapter Thirteen

"Get out of my way!" Winston shouted, honking at the slow car in front of him. *The play starts in five minutes—I'm never going to make it there in time.* Winston gripped the steering wheel with white-knuckled anxiety.

He was just barely able to convince Amanda to put her cellular phone away before she could make any damaging calls. If Amanda had told her husband that Winston had been stalking her, Winston was sure that the dean would be likely to believe it. Now he knew that his last and only hope was to speak to the dean himself.

The car ahead of him pulled over to the side of the road, and Winston slammed his foot down on the gas pedal, watching the needle on the speedometer move way beyond the speed limit. Winston drove even faster as the little orange VW Beetle skidded around a curve. *Four minutes.* He squeezed the steering wheel in his hands.

There was only one way to take all the sting out of Amanda's threats and get the alibi Winston so desperately needed. He had to disarm Amanda entirely and tell Dean Franklin the truth to his face. The dean himself said he wanted to help—not knowing, of course, what exactly he would be getting himself into. But Winston had to take the risk. *I'm not going to prison for Amanda,* he swore to himself.

Winston brought the car to a screeching halt right in front of the theater and jumped out, still leaving the engine running. Scores of well-dressed people were crowding into the front entrance. Winston rudely pushed past them in his ripped jeans and sneakers, scanning the plush, red-carpeted lobby for Dean Franklin and Amanda.

"Hey—watch it!" someone yelled at Winston as he wove in and out of the line into the theater.

An older woman scowled at him with indignation. "Who let *him* in here?"

Winston ignored the commotion around him, determined to get to the dean before the curtain went up. But black-tied ushers flanked every entrance to the theater.

"Excuse me, sir," Winston said, poking one of the men on the shoulder.

The usher lifted his nose in distaste, grimacing

at Winston's jean jacket. "How may I help you?"

"Sorry to bug you—but I have this pet monkey; his name is Macbeth—"

The usher stared at him in horror. Winston had read somewhere that it was bad luck to say the name Macbeth in a theater, and judging from his reaction, Winston could tell this usher was superstitious.

Winston continued. "So I was walking by the theater with Macbeth on my shoulder, when all of a sudden he jumps off and runs in here. You haven't seen him, have you?"

"Young man," the usher said harshly, "the performance begins in two minutes. I suggest you find him quickly. We will not tolerate wild animals running around here."

"I understand," Winston said, looking over the crowd. He pointed suddenly, as if he spotted his imaginary pet. "I think I see him! Macbeth! Macbeth!"

The usher cringed and let Winston past the velvet ropes. He found himself standing in the back of the first-floor orchestra section. If the dean and Amanda weren't sitting down there, he had three other balconies to check.

Where are you? Winston's eyes methodically glanced at every seat, his heart slamming against his ribs. What was he going to say when he finally did catch up with the dean? *Don't think about that right now,* Winston told himself. *Just concentrate on finding him*.

And then he did. Actually it was Amanda he spotted first, in an aisle seat about halfway down. She was wearing the same blue-green gown that had stopped Winston's heart on the night of the party, but this time she looked different. Maybe it was the yellow light from the chandelier above, instead of the silvery moonlight, that transformed her. No longer was she a mystical creature—now she had sickly aura about her. Her greed was starting to show.

Blocking out thoughts of both the future and the past, Winston felt himself being submerged in the moment. *This is your last chance,* he thought, taking decisive steps down the aisle, staring at the back of the dean's head. Time seemed to slow down as Winston's senses buzzed with heightened perception. This was going to be the most important moment of his life. His entire future depended on its outcome.

Four rows away. Winston had opened his mouth to call to the dean when Amanda started to turn her head, looking up the aisle. She saw him. Winston's throat closed. Amanda shook her head in slow motion and leaned over to her husband, saying something. Then she stood up. She walked up the aisle toward him. Winston's pulse thundered in his ears. Time resumed its normal speed. The houselights flickered as a warning that the play was about to start.

Amanda roughly grabbed Winston's arm and pulled him with her to the back of the theater.

"How many times do I have to tell you to leave me alone?" she demanded, glaring at him.

Winston leaned against the wall, staring her down. "I didn't come to see you; I came to see your husband."

"Well, I don't think he wants to see you right now."

"Why not?" Winston, infuriated, jammed his shaking hands into the pockets of his blue jeans. "What did you tell him, Amanda?"

In the dark corner near the side exit Amanda pressed her hands flirtatiously against Winston's chest. "That you've been stalking me, of course," she said with an evil giggle.

Winston grabbed Amanda forcefully by the wrists in a fit of rage. "How could you tell him that?" Winston cried incredulously. "I thought we had a deal!" Winston ran a quaking hand through his hair, trying desperately to find a way out of the corner Amanda had backed him into. "You've ruined my life!" he hissed through clenched teeth. "Believe me, Amanda, I'm going to make sure that everyone—and I mean *everyone*—knows what you have done."

"You're hurting me!" Amanda said, loud enough so that a nearby usher turned his head toward them. "If I were in your position, I wouldn't be making idle threats."

"This is no idle threat." Winston stared down at her, ignoring the usher, who was moving closer. "Even if I get sent to prison, I'm going to make sure that your husband finds out everything." He dropped her wrists.

"Is there a problem, miss?" the usher asked, keeping his eye on Winston.

"Everything is under control, thank you," she answered. The usher, who seemed unconvinced, stood close by. Amanda tossed back her hair and gave Winston a haughty smile. "My, my, Winston, how you've changed in a few weeks. You were just a pathetic, spineless little boy when I met you, and now you seem to have it all figured out."

The houselights flickered again. The usher stepped forward. "Please take your seats."

Winston ignored him. "I haven't had much of a choice," he said to Amanda. "It seems as though everyone else is controlling my life right now."

Amanda moved in close until her lips were only a fraction of an inch away from his. "That was your fatal mistake. You should never let anyone gain power over you," she whispered. As she backed away, her lips curved into a wry smile. "Welcome to adulthood, Winston," she said, blowing him a kiss. "You're on your own."

"Excuse me, are you Paul?"

Paul turned around and smiled at the fellow

usher who was approaching him. The usher was wearing a tuxedo just like his own; it was the same standard-issue tuxedo that all the theater ushers wore. "Yes, that's me," Paul said.

The other usher smiled and extended his hand. "I'm David," he said, introducing himself. "There's a call for you at the front desk. It's your wife."

Paul grinned in embarrassment. "Helen— I've told her never to call me at work. But she keeps doing it anyway."

"That's all right," David said. "Go ahead and take it."

"I can't leave my post."

David leaned against the door to the side entrance. "I'll cover for you. I'm on break, and I won't tell anyone."

"Are you sure?" Paul asked.

"It's no problem."

Paul smiled gratefully. "Watch out for the guy in the corner, David," he whispered under his breath, pointing out a young man in ripped jeans who had been arguing with a beautiful blond woman in an evening gown just a few yards away. "He looks like trouble."

David nodded and stepped aside as Paul went into the lobby to get his phone call. The houselights dimmed and the red velvet curtain raised, revealing a stage designed to look like an outdoor café in Paris. Out of the corner of his eye the usher watched the couple standing near the back exit. The rough-looking young man disappeared out the exit door, and the beautiful blond started to walk down the aisle toward her seat.

"Excuse me, madam, but you must wait until the scene is over," he said, gently touching her arm. Without even glancing at him, the woman obligingly stood beside him in the shadows as the play began.

With his hands clasped behind his back the usher looked down, smiled to himself, and clicked together the heels of his cowboy boots in the darkness.

Winston walked out the back exit, taking the path that curved around to the front where his car was parked. Never in his life had he felt so absolutely hopeless. His body felt like an empty shell, devoid of all feeling and expectation. The only thing he had left to do was to throw himself upon the mercy of the detectives. He'd tell them everything, even though he had no proof of any kind, and Amanda would deny it all. *I wish you still loved me, Denise,* Winston thought painfully. *This would be so much easier if you still loved me.*

Making his way through the rows of expensive cars, Winston noticed a truck parked near the back. The raised wheels, pinstriping, and floodlights running across the top were strangely out of place next to the glossy imports. An icy shiver coursed through Winston as his eyes fell on the license plate. BABY.

"Oh no—he's here!" Winston turned on his heels and bolted back toward the theater. It was an unusual spot for Jackson Lowe to be searching for his next victim. *That could only mean one thing,* Winston thought in terror. Jackson somehow must have known that Amanda was the real witness. And the only way he could stop her from testifying was to kill her.

"You can't go in there!" the distinguished-looking man at the entrance shouted as Winston plowed through the front doors of the lobby and headed straight for the theater. "The play has started!"

Winston's breathing was erratic as bursts of adrenaline exploded into his system. *Where is she? I've got to find her.* He threw open the doors and shoved past the ushers who were in pursuit. Sweat poured in rivers down his back as he glanced down the center aisle of the dark orchestra section. Amanda's seat was empty. *Did she ever make it back to her seat?*

Winston ran along the back wall, gasping for breath, heads turning in his direction as he whipped past. A murmur ran through the crowd. He had to find Amanda before it was too late.

Amanda was standing in the same spot where he left her; an usher was turned toward her. The usher's arms seemed to be moving rapidly, flying

211

in the darkness. Winston roughly grabbed the usher by the shoulder, catching a glimpse of a rattlesnake tail on his wrist. Jackson turned around and smiled at Winston, the flashing glint of his steel blade reflecting in his eyes.

"She's all yours, buddy," Jackson said, dropping the butcher knife on the floor and slipping out the back exit.

Amanda sank to the floor, her blue-green evening gown shredded and stained with dark blood. Winston held her urgently in his arms and tried in vain to keep her head from rolling back. Pressing two fingers against her neck, he could feel no pulse. He sucked in an audible breath. "Oh, Amanda, he got to you too!" Winston cried, feeling the sticky, warm ooze of Amanda's blood soaking into his own shirt.

"There's been a murder!" someone screamed. The houselights suddenly came up. Chaos broke out as people ran in all directions, scrambling for the nearest exit.

Temporarily blocked by the pandemonium, the ushers fought against the crowd to reach Winston. He looked down at the knife lying by his feet and the fresh, crimson blood staining his hands. *I have to get out of here.*

Winston eased Amanda's lifeless body to the floor, then hurdled the first row of seats.

"That's him! That's the killer!" a man shouted across the room, pointing to Winston.

Winston ran down a narrow side aisle, then cut across an empty row, moving toward the center. That was when he came face-to-face with Dean Franklin.

Their eyes locked for a moment—Winston's wild with terror, the dean's filled with confusion.

"I swear I didn't do it," Winston said quickly.

The dean stood only an arm's length away, close enough to grasp Winston's arm and detain him. But he didn't move.

One of the ushers started gaining on Winston, and he took off again. Winston leaped onto the stage, scattering actors as he crashed through the set. Working his way through the maze backstage, he finally found the fire exit. Pushing open the door with his bloody hands, Winston ran out into the dark night, never stopping to look back.

Denise gasped in horror when she opened her door to find Winston, pale, shaking, and covered with blood, leaning against the wall. "Winston! Are you hurt?"

"No," Winston gasped. His hair was plastered to his sweat-soaked face. He was trembling.

Denise helped him inside, bolting the door behind her. The rage she'd felt earlier was dissolved by the simple fact that she still loved him. Denise demanded no explanation from him at the moment——her only concern was that he was going to be all right.

"I'm not going to stay," Winston said, the words coming out stiffly as he tried to catch his breath. "Jackson killed Amanda right after I begged her to go to the police and tell them everything. He ran off and left me alone with the body. Even Dean Franklin saw me. Now everyone really *will* think I'm the killer."

"Oh no . . ." Denise covered her mouth, tears streaming down her face. "I'm sure if you talk to the detectives——"

"They have a mountain of circumstantial evidence linking me to the murders," Winston said, collapsing onto a chair. "The only person who could clear my name is dead. It's not looking good for me, Denise."

Falling to the floor, Denise rested her head in Winston's lap and cried. He stroked her head with gentle hands. How could anyone possibly mistake him for a brutal murderer? Winston was the kindest, sweetest person she had ever met.

"I don't have a lot of time," he said in a shaky voice.

A deep yearning wrenched inside Denise as she mourned the life they would never have together. Before their world had been turned upside down, she had always thought that Winston was the man she would spend the rest of her life with. He was the one she wanted to buy a house with, have a family with; the one to be by her side through everything. Hot, fresh, painful tears coursed down Denise's cheeks, soaking into the cloth of Winston's jeans. It would have been a good life.

"I came by to apologize again. I'm so sorry, Denise," Winston said thickly. His fingertips softly grazed her cheek. "And to tell you how much I love you. I'll always love you."

Denise turned her swollen face toward him. "I love you too, Winston—in spite of everything." She kissed his palm. "I can't help it."

"Before I go, I need to ask something of you," Winston said. "Please promise me that someday you'll find it in your heart to forgive me. I know it's too soon right now, but someday I'm hoping you'll realize that I never meant to hurt you. It was a terrible mistake, and I'm going to pay for it for the rest of my life."

Denise stared up at Winston's troubled face and looked deeply into his eyes. "I can't make a promise like that—I don't know if I'll ever be able to forgive you. But I *can* promise you that I'll try."

Winston nodded silently, as if he knew that he couldn't ask for anything more.

"Winnie, where are you going to go?"

"I don't know," he murmured. "I was thinking Mexico."

"You shouldn't run away," she said. "You'll look guilty."

"And if I stay, I'll still look guilty," Winston argued. "There isn't much of a choice."

Denise brushed Winston's hair out of his eyes. "Why don't you stay and rest before you go? Maybe we can come up with a way to get you out of this."

"I don't want to get you involved," he said.

"I'm already involved," Denise answered gently. "Stay a little while longer in case I come up with an idea."

Winston leaned his head back and closed his eyes. "All right," he murmured softly. "Just for a little while."

Chapter
Fourteen

Elizabeth and Winston waited silently in the living room of the beach house while Denise changed in the bedroom. Staring up at the wall clock, Elizabeth watched the seconds tick by like an eternity, her heartbeat increasing with each minute that passed. Every single nerve in Elizabeth's body had been on edge from the very moment Denise and Winston had called to say they'd come up with a plan to trap Jackson Lowe. Elizabeth had jumped into her Jeep and had driven over to the house as fast as she could, willing to do whatever it took to clear Winston's name and to see that Jackson Lowe went to prison.

I hope we know what we're doing, Elizabeth thought fearfully. *There are so many things that could go wrong.* She jumped up suddenly and slid open the glass door leading to the deck, hoping the fresh sea air would clear away the negative thoughts that kept tugging at the corners of her brain.

Winston was sitting on the white couch, feet tapping impatiently on the hardwood floor. He shifted his body nervously from one side to the other, tortured sighs rising up from his throat every few moments.

"I don't like this," he finally said.

Elizabeth pulled a screen across the door and breathed in the salty air. "None of us do, Winston, but we don't have much of a choice."

The tips of Winston's fingers sank deep into a nearby throw pillow. "I'd rather go to jail than put Denise in danger."

Elizabeth looked out over the soft sand and beyond to the horizon, where the red-orange sun was beginning to spread itself over the greenish blue water. Usually Elizabeth treasured the beautiful colors of the setting sun, but on this particular night the red glow looked ominous, sending shivers down her spine.

"We're not going to let you go to jail for something you didn't do, Winston." Elizabeth exhaled, returning to the couch. She touched Winston's arm gently. "The only thing you're guilty of is having a fling with Amanda—she's the reason you're in this mess."

Winston's eyes were glassy, distant. "There's no point in blaming her now," he said solemnly, staring out at the beach. "I hope Dean Franklin is doing OK."

"I hope so too," Elizabeth answered in a whisper, her eyes fixated on the setting sun.

The door to the bedroom creaked open, snapping both Winston and Elizabeth out of their reverie. Denise strode across the living room and stood directly in front of the two of them.

"How do I look?" she asked, hands planted firmly on hips as she batted her mile-long fake eyelashes.

"That does it." Winston shook his head, bounding out of his seat and pacing the room in tight circles. "I can't let you do this."

"Don't freak out on me now, Winnie," Denise answered, following him. Her black spike heels clicked against the floor as she walked. "I'm doing it, and that's final!"

Elizabeth looked at Denise's getup and felt an icy chill of apprehension. *Maybe Winston's right*. The short black spandex skirt and skimpy red tank top made up the kind of sleazy outfit that would definitely attract the killer's attention. *But what happens after that?* Elizabeth thought worriedly.

Winston turned his back to them and looked out at the beach. "I can't put you in that kind of danger, Denise."

Denise folded her arms across her chest with determination, her heavily glossed red lips curving into a frown. "Are *you* with me, Liz?"

Against her better judgment, Elizabeth nodded. "I'm in."

"We're going after Lowe whether you like it or not," Denise said fearlessly. "And I'd feel a whole lot better if you were there, Winnie, to back us up."

Elizabeth shoved back the anxiety that continued to nag at her. The plan was risky, but they had to take the chance. They had to make sure the true killer paid for his crime. "We need you, Winston," she said.

Winston nodded reluctantly, still unable to look in Denise's direction. "Have we figured out how this is going to work yet?"

"Pretty much, except for a few small details." Elizabeth stood up and put her arm supportively around Denise's shoulders. "We can figure out the rest in the car."

"What about a wig?" Winston asked. "Do you have a blond wig? He likes blondes."

"I borrowed a long blond one from one of the Theta sisters." Denise gave Elizabeth a hesitant smile. Elizabeth could see the slightest flicker of fear deep in Denise's eyes. "Are we all ready to go?" Denise asked.

"We should use my Jeep," Elizabeth said, feeling for the keys in the pocket of her jeans. "The police are probably looking for Winston's car."

Outside, the sun was well below the horizon

and dusk was beginning to fall. Elizabeth took a deep breath, trying to turn her attention away from the pounding of her heart to the pounding surf. But not even the sound of the crashing ocean waves could cool the panic that sizzled in her blood.

"Winnie, are you ready?" Denise asked, tossing a hairbrush and some makeup into a big straw bag.

Winston turned around slowly, his shoulders drooping. His eyes were sunk deep in their sockets, reflecting darkly the anguish he'd been in for days. "Denise, I'm scared," he murmured.

"I know, honey," Denise answered, her voice tense. "We all are."

"Still no sign of his truck yet," Elizabeth called over her shoulder as she turned the Jeep left onto the main drag.

From the backseat Winston peered out the window, looking at all the local dives and darkened storefronts they passed. There was only a handful of bars around, and Jackson had to be at one of them. "I wonder if the guy's left town," he thought aloud.

"No way." Denise, who was sitting next to Winston on the bench seat, shook her head. "Now that you're the main suspect, I'm sure Jackson Lowe isn't going anywhere."

Winston balled his sweaty hands into tight fists. The orange streetlights flashed like a

221

strobe light inside the dark vehicle as they rolled on through the night. *It's a crazy world,* Winston thought, his mind on the verge of exploding. No matter how hard he tried, Winston still couldn't comprehend how an innocent guy like himself could be blamed for murders he didn't commit while the real criminal went free. It was like the world had been turned completely upside down and inside out.

Denise placed her warm hand on his, as if she could read his mind. "You're going to drive yourself crazy, Winnie. Don't think about it. I need you here one hundred percent."

Winston looked at her, watching the orange shadows move across her stoic face. She was right. Now was not the time to think. He had to act.

"Jackson hates flirtatious women—but only if they're flirting with other men," Winston said, continuing his instruction on the likes and dislikes of the killer. He wanted Denise to know everything. "Don't pay any attention to him. Just flirt with whoever happens to be nearby."

Denise tugged at the hem of her tiny skirt. "Man, this guy sounds like a real nut job."

"Oh—and make sure you order a drink," Winston added. "A real drink, so they don't get suspicious."

Reaching under the seat, Denise opened her

straw bag and took out the blond wig. Winston rubbed an artificial lock between his fingers. It was fine and elastic like doll's hair. Anyone could tell it wasn't real. Denise twisted her dark curls into a bun, then leaned far forward. When the wig was secured, she threw her head back, letting the fake tresses cascade down her shoulders.

"Do you like?" she teased, puckering her lips.

"It's pretty—in a trampy sort of way," Winston answered, daring to let himself grin a little for the first time in days.

Denise tossed a long blond strand over one shoulder like a beauty queen. "That's the nicest thing you could've said to me!"

Even when her life is in danger, she can laugh about it, Winston thought with deep admiration. Denise had to be one of the bravest people he had ever met. No matter what the circumstances were, she always rose to the occasion with hurricane force. Even after all he'd put her through, Denise was there for him, stronger than ever.

The stoplight ahead turned red and Elizabeth brought the Jeep to a rolling stop. She looked around. "I still don't see him—it's been almost an hour."

"Let's give it some more time," Denise said, straightening her wig. "Besides, we could use the time to go over the plan."

Going over the plan again in his mind, Winston reworked the details, thinking of possible snags. "You know, Denise, I was thinking—maybe Elizabeth should go in with you."

Denise shook her big, blond hairdo. "It'll look too suspicious, with me dressed up and Liz in normal clothes. Let's just leave the plan the way it is—both you and Elizabeth waiting for me outside the bar, watching through the window from across the street."

"What if he picks a place where we can't see in?" Winston asked, knowing they had to cover every possible scenario.

Denise sighed. "Stop worrying, Winnie! We'll deal with it if and when it happens." She pulled out a tube of red lipstick and put on a second heavy coat. "You both will be waiting for me in the Jeep, right?"

"Right," Winston answered. Opening his fists, Winston rubbed his wet palms on the front of his jeans. "You go in the bar, get Jackson's attention, then leave alone, so he'll follow you out."

Elizabeth looked at them in the rearview mirror. "Give us the thumbs-up sign, Denise, so we know everything is going as planned."

"Then I keep walking," Denise said. "Which direction do I go?"

"Pick the one that goes to the least-populated area," Winston said. "Walk slowly so that Jackson will have a chance to catch up to you. Once he starts following, don't look back—just keep on going. We'll be there to back you up."

Elizabeth nodded. "We're going to stay close by. Either Winston or I will call the detectives from a nearby pay phone."

Denise touched up her heavy eye makeup. "So if all goes as planned, the police will arrive on the scene before I do any serious damage to Mr. Lowe."

A wry grin twisted Winston's lips. "Jackson Lowe will be in the safety of police custody faster than you can blink your fake lashes."

The Jeep came to a sudden, screeching halt as Elizabeth slammed on the brakes. "There he is!"

Winston pressed his face against the back window. "Where?"

"He drove right by me, heading west!" Elizabeth slammed the stick shift in reverse and backed into a nearby driveway before reversing direction and following in pursuit. "Hang on, guys!"

Winston and Denise fell silent. *I hope this doesn't turn out to be another huge mistake,* he thought, trying to swallow the hard lump of apprehension that was lodged in his windpipe. Tenderly he reached across the bench seat and touched the top of Denise's hand. She stared straight ahead, watching the dark road and the red taillights of Jackson's truck, her eyes wide and frightened. Denise opened her hand and laced her fingers with his, holding tightly.

The chase ended a few minutes later when Jackson Lowe and BABY decided to stop by the Lizard Lounge, directly in the center of town. It was a dingy bar with an exterior of chipping red paint and dirty window glass, nestled between an abandoned diner and a dirt parking lot. Jackson turned into the lot, his speeding truck fishtailing in the sand, leaving behind a cloud of dust.

Elizabeth parallel-parked the Jeep on the main road, directly across the street from the bar. It was a safe distance from the killer and was a perfect lookout point.

"He's gutsy," Denise said as they watched Jackson jump out of the truck and stroll inside the bar. "The police station can't be more than a half mile from here."

"He has nothing to worry about—everyone thinks it's me," Winston said, eyeing the green neon lizard glowing above the front door. His heart was already beginning to hammer loudly in his chest.

Elizabeth turned off the engine. "The front window's pretty big. We should be able to see in OK," she said with a tense sigh. "And there's a pay phone on the corner."

"As soon as you leave the bar, start walking toward the residential area," Winston said,

226

pointing to the sidewalk near the parking lot. Beyond the lot the landscape suddenly changed into a grassy neighborhood with clusters of trees and bushes. A quarter mile down the road there were a few houses.

"Got it," Denise said energetically. Winston was starting to feel queasy, and she gave him a sympathetic look as if she could read his mind. "Don't worry, Winnie—everything is going to be just fine," she said, lightly kissing the tip of his nose.

"Be careful, Denise—" he choked.

Elizabeth unbuckled her seat belt. "We don't have a lot of time. Are you guys ready?"

Denise gave them a thumbs-up sign. "Let's do it!"

As soon as Denise opened the door to the bar she was blasted with a thick blue cloud of cigarette smoke and the noisy riffs of guitar rock. *What am I getting myself into?* she wondered, trying to breathe through the suffocating smoke. Every guy in the place stopped whatever they were doing and stared at Denise, as if some silent alarm had gone off the minute she walked through the door. Denise sauntered in, a seductive smile hiding the tumultuous mix of fear, horror, and embarrassment that roiled inside her. Giving her blond wig a confident shake, she cruised over toward the bar.

What's the matter with you, bozo? Never seen a

woman before? she shouted silently at the beer-guzzling creep who licked his chops as she walked by. Denise bit down hard on the tip of her tongue and smiled, swaying her hips in time to the song that blared from the jukebox in the corner.

"Would you look at that?" A guy in a sweat-stained T-shirt gawked at Denise as she walked by, leaning over the pool table with a dim green light-bulb suspended over it. "That is *beau-ti-ful.*"

The guy's paunchy sidekick let out a low whistle as he chalked up his pool cue. He laughed. "Don't you look at that, Larry—you'll go blind!"

Denise winked at both of them and giggled, fighting an urgent need to vomit. *If Elizabeth and Winston are watching me half as closely as these two are, I have nothing to worry about,* she thought, wriggling past the pool table.

Jackson Lowe was already seated at the end of the bar, a shot of whiskey gripped in each hand. *That's my man.* Denise slithered up to the bar, smiling at the leering stares, feeling her flesh crawl with each catcall.

Denise took a seat a few stools down from the killer, strategically adjusting her skirt so that it wasn't too revealing. Crossing her legs, she casually looked around. The TV set bolted to the wall was showing a basketball game with the sound turned off. Denise couldn't help noticing that she was the only woman in the entire place, except for a wrinkled old lady who was sitting in the corner, drinking straight from a bottle of tequila.

"What does a girl have to do to get a drink around here?" Denise said breathlessly, licking her lips at the greasy-looking bartender. Her heart thumped against her rib cage.

"Hey, Teddy!" one of the pool players yelled to the bartender. "Did you see what just came in?"

Teddy smiled at Denise, revealing the brown stumps of several missing bottom teeth. "How can I miss a pretty lady like that?" he asked, his greasy little eyes traveling down her body and back up again. "What'll it be, pretty lady?"

It was impossible to decide from the enormous collection of bottles that lined the wall. Denise didn't know one drink from the next. "What do you suggest?" she said in a playful voice loud enough for Jackson to hear.

Teddy grinned. "I got a special kind of whiskey that just came in—you want to give it a try?"

"Sure," Denise cooed, tossing her hair over one shoulder. Her scalp was hot and itchy under the wig. "I'll try anything once."

While Teddy poured her a drink, Denise slid off the stool and walked over to the jukebox in the corner, making eyes at every man who crossed her path. But even with all the attention Denise was creating, Jackson still wasn't looking at her. *Come on,* Denise thought impatiently. *Look over here so I can get out of this creepy place.*

"I like that skirt!" someone yelled from across the room.

With shaking fingers, Denise pulled a handful of change out of her tiny purse and starting feeding the jukebox. Her fingertips viciously punched the numbers at random, her mind too focused on what was going on behind her to pay any attention to the music.

"Hi there, sweetie," drawled someone standing a few feet away.

It's him. Denise spun around on her high heels. She'd expected to be standing face-to-face with Jackson, but instead she found herself staring up at a six-foot-five biker, complete with overgrown beard, leather vest, and two tattoos. One meaty bicep was decorated with a picture of a naked woman, and the other was covered with something that looked like an octopus.

"Hey there," Denise answered, pouting her lips. It took all the strength she had not to run right out of the bar, screaming at the top of her lungs.

The biker smiled, giving Denise a glimpse of his tobacco-stained teeth. "You alone?"

"You bet," Denise answered.

"I'm Squid," he said, pointing to the tattoo

on his left arm to illustrate the point.

"I'm—" Denise stopped. She'd forgotten to come up with a fake name. Looking at the patch on Squid's leather jacket, she suddenly had a burst of inspiration. "Harley—my name is Harley."

Squid's eyes bulged. "You're kidding."

Denise shook her head. "My parents used to ride."

"I've never met anyone with a name like that," he answered, his eyes narrowing.

Before Squid had a chance to get suspicious, an old rock tune came over the jukebox, and Denise squealed with glee. She grabbed his wrists and danced around him. "I just *love* this song! Don't you, Squid?"

"What's going on in there?" Winston asked, kicking the toe of his sneaker against the back of the passenger seat. "Hasn't she been in there long enough already?"

Using the sleeve of her blue button-down shirt, Elizabeth tried to wipe away a patch of fog on the Jeep's window. She pressed her face to the glass, but all she could see was a hazy green fog inside the bar. "I can't tell what's going on in there, Winston, but you know she's trying to get out of there as fast as she can."

"It's not fast enough." Winston punched the back of the seat. "This is really freaking me out."

"Take it easy—everything's going to be OK," Elizabeth answered, not only to calm Winston but also to make herself feel better. She looked at the clock on the dashboard. Denise had been inside for twenty minutes already and there was no sign that she was going to come out anytime soon.

Winston covered his face with his hands. "I don't know, Liz. I just have a really bad feeling about this."

"Winston, stop it!" Elizabeth shouted. "Panicking is not going to help the situation any. Denise is the one whose life is in danger, and she's more together than the two of us combined."

Leaning forward, Winston pressed his cheek against the headrest and closed his eyes. "She's so amazing," he said with a sigh. "I can't let anything happen to her."

"Nothing's going to happen if we stay calm and alert. We have to be ready to get the detectives the second she steps out of that door." Elizabeth peered out the window again, but there was still no sign of Denise. A sleek black Harley-Davidson motorcycle gleamed under the streetlight in front of the bar, sending up electrifying ripples of fear from Elizabeth's tailbone to the top of her scalp. *What kind of men are in there?* she wondered. *Is Denise really all right?*

"I don't like this at all," Winston moaned, his voice rising a frightful octave. "It was a stupid idea to let her go in there alone."

"There are lots of people in there," Elizabeth countered. She sat on her hands to keep them from shaking. "She'll be walking out any minute now."

Winston's fingertips dug into the seat cushion; his eyes were wild. "And then what? The serial killer will follow her and drag her into the bushes? You know what's going to happen if Jackson gets his hands on her, don't you? He's going to take out one of his butcher knives and he's going to kill her!"

"Stop talking like that!" Elizabeth shouted, covering her ears with her hands. The terror that had been building inside her since they left the beach house threatened to unleash itself with a lion's fury. There *were* too many things that could go wrong, there *were* too many dangers, but the fact of the matter was that they were already too deep into the plan to back out now. Any move they tried to make that wasn't according to plan could end up plunging them into even more jeopardy.

Elizabeth rolled down the window and deeply inhaled the fresh air. As her head cleared she pushed back her fear and concentrated on the job at hand. "Listen up, Winston, because I'm only going to say this one more time." She peeled his white-knuckled fingers off the edge of the seat and didn't continue until he made eye contact with her. "Denise needs you right now. I know you're scared, but you have to be tough. Nothing's going to happen to her as long as you and I are on top of things. We're not going to let Jackson lay a finger on her."

Wiping his brow with his forearm, Winston forced a weak smile. "You're right, Liz," he answered, staring out the window. "If Jackson wants to hurt Denise, he's going to have to kill me first."

Chapter Fifteen

Jackson Lowe tossed back his third whiskey, watching the drama that was unfolding in the corner near the jukebox. The blond, who called herself Harley, seemed to be making a lot of friends. *Disgusting little tramp.* Harley was rolling her hips and shaking that sexy blond hair of hers, not caring that practically every guy in the joint was wagging his tongue at her like a drooling dog.

"I want another," Jackson told the bartender, pushing the empty shot glass across the bar. The alcohol was slipping through his system like quicksilver. While the bartender poured, Jackson's eyes were transfixed by Harley as she let that freak named Squid run his hands up and down her body. Her long legs, her golden hair—they were just like Gina's. Jackson shivered convulsively with disgust. *She's nothing but a cheap floozy. They all are.*

The bartender handed him a full shot glass and Jackson threw two bills down on the counter, still staring at the sleaze show in the corner. "Tell me something," Jackson asked, feeling for his cigarettes. "Are there any nice girls left in this world?"

"You don't think *she's* nice?" the bartender asked, leering with the best of them.

"No, I don't." Jackson lit his cigarette, his upper lip curling in a sneer. *Sad sack, he doesn't know what a nice girl is,* Jackson thought. *He doesn't know what it's like to have a beautiful, perfect angel by his side. The only pure angel left on earth, meant only for you.*

"Well, I think she's pretty nice," the bartender said, leaning against the bar. "And I bet if you were nice to her, she'd be *real nice* to you." He gave Jackson a confidential wink.

Pig. It was guys like him who turned the angels into filthy pieces of trash. Blowing a thin stream of smoke in the air, Jackson watched Harley dance in slow, seductive circles. Even under the layers of thick makeup, he could see that she had once been an angel too. Innocence flickered in her eyes like a dying flame. It wasn't too late. *I can still save her,* Jackson thought, taking another drag from his cigarette. *Just like I saved Gina.*

"Oh, Squid, you're so silly!" Harley

giggled, pushing him away with a teasing smile on her face. The song ended, and Harley broke through the circle of men, heading toward the bar. "It's hot in here—I need a drink."

"Got your whiskey right here," Teddy said, smacking the counter with an eager hand.

Harley smiled and slid onto the stool right next to Jackson. She winked at him. "What are you drinking there, cowboy?" she asked, pointing to his empty shot glass.

Jackson stared at Harley, unblinking. His veins pulsed at the thought of drawing his sharp blade across her long, slender throat, her screams of terror rising up as she begged for mercy. It was so beautiful to watch them beg for their lives—all the ugliness seemed to fall away, revealing the angel underneath. *It's too late, Gina,* Jackson had said when she fell to her knees. *You're tainted, ruined forever.* Jackson remembered the tears of joy that had come to his eyes as he freed Gina's angelic spirit from the snare of her evil body.

"This one is a talker, huh?" Harley said sarcastically, loud enough for everyone to hear. She shot Jackson a haughty look.

Squid's face turned mean. He didn't seem to like the idea that his tramp was talking to someone else. "Drink!" he ordered, pointing to Harley's shot glass.

Harley giggled stupidly. "Oh, right," she

answered, putting the glass to her lips and tilting back her head.

Enjoy your drink, Jackson thought as he watched Harley drain the glass. His fingers touched his back pocket, feeling the solid, thrilling contour of his hunting knife. *It's going to be your last.*

Oh, boy, does this stuff burn. Denise struggled not to cough as she finished the whiskey. It was like drinking liquid fire. *I can't believe people drink this stuff for fun.* Everyone in the bar, including Jackson, was staring at her. Denise turned the shot glass upside down and slammed it triumphantly on the bar like a pro.

"Get her another!" Squid shouted, throwing a few bills at Teddy.

Denise held up her hand. "No, thanks, sweetie," she wheezed through the burn. "I'm fine."

Squid took a strand of her blond hair between his fingers and rubbed it. "Make it a double," he said to the bartender.

Just great. Denise smiled through gritted teeth, feeling the hot whiskey settle in her veins. The only reason she even had the drink was to get out of dancing with Squid, and now he was trying to get her drunk. *This was a very, very bad idea,* she thought, a feeling of prickly panic rising inside her. Being the only woman in a bar crowded with rabid men who plied her with liquor was probably even more dangerous than being alone with Jackson Lowe.

"Here you are, my dear," Teddy said, plunking two shots of whiskey in front of Denise.

She stared down at the drinks, her stomach lurching violently at the thought of drinking more. *Get out of here,* whispered a little voice inside Denise's head. Jackson was still staring at her with a blood-chilling look in his eye. *You have his attention; now just make a break for it.*

Sliding off the stool, Denise flashed everyone a blinding smile. "Thanks for the drinks," she said huskily. "But I have to get going."

Squid raised his thick, hairy arm and blocked her. "Where?"

"I have to get home—my husband is expecting me," she said sheepishly.

Jackson slammed his shot glass angrily on the counter, his gaze still fixed on her.

Denise swallowed hard. "My husband's going to be really upset if I'm late."

"I just bought you a drink." Squid's arm was still blocking her way. "Don't you want it?"

"I've had enough, thanks," Denise said, attempting to squeeze around him.

Squid stepped in front of Denise and handed her one of the shot glasses. He picked up the second shot and held it in the air. "You're not going anywhere until you drink."

Denise's stomach heaved. "Really, I can't—"

The guys standing around the pool table started chanting, "Har-ley! Har-ley!" and clapping in rhythm.

Squid clinked his glass against hers as if he were making a toast. "Bottoms up!" he said with booming laugh, then knocked his shot back in one gulp.

It looks like I'm not leaving until I drink, Denise said to herself, sniffing the potent brown liquid. A wave of nausea hit her. She raised the glass and drank, feeling the sting as the liquor trickled down her throat.

"Yeah, Harley!" one of the guys shouted.

Denise steadied herself against the bar, feeling a little light-headed. At that moment she would have given anything for a glass of water to put out the fire in her stomach. *I have to get out of here,* she thought sluggishly.

"Thanks, Squid—it was a blast." Denise patted him on the shoulder. Her lips felt tingly, as if they were turning numb. "I gotta go."

At that very moment a slow, syrupy ballad came on the jukebox. "No," Squid said, blocking Denise's way again. "We're going to dance."

Despite the loose, rubbery feeling that was seeping into her muscles, Denise was starting to feel a very real sense of panic. She was trapped by Squid's enormous frame as he stopped her from making a run for the door.

Even if she could have somehow made it past him, there were fifteen other slimeballs she still had to dodge. There was no way out.

"Good song," Squid grunted. He pulled her toward the jukebox and took her into his furry arms, squeezing her tightly.

Denise's cheek was pressed against him, the grimy smell of motorcycle oil and sweat wafting up from his leather vest. She could feel the blazing stare of Jackson's eyes searing into her back. Over Squid's shoulder Denise glanced out the dirty window at the front of the bar, spotting Elizabeth's bright red Jeep across the street.

How am I going to get out of here? Denise wondered helplessly. Squid held her tighter as they spun in slow circles, the keys hooked to his belt loop digging deeply into her side.

"You're with me now," Squid breathed into her hair. "Don't even *think* about leaving."

"I'm going in," Winston said, pushing the passenger seat forward. "It's taking way too long for her to come out. I know something's wrong."

"It's too soon to go in," Elizabeth said, holding him back.

"It's been a half hour, Liz. I'm calling the police."

"Wait a few more minutes." The flutter in Elizabeth's voice told Winston she was just as afraid

241

as he was. "If we call now before Jackson does anything, the police won't arrest him," she argued. "You'll be in just as much trouble as before."

Winston's head pounded, feeling like there were two sledgehammers coming at him from both sides. His gaze remained fixed on the door of the bar. "What if Denise is in trouble?"

"I'm sure she's fine. Denise is tough."

Winston wasn't convinced. "I don't care how tough she is; no one can fight off twenty or thirty drunken guys at once."

Elizabeth nodded, resting her head on the steering wheel. "Let's wait three more minutes. We're so close, Winston. I hate to see us lose our last chance at clearing your name."

Winston opened the door and jumped out of the Jeep. "I've lost just about everything in my life over this mess. I'm not about to lose Denise too," he said resolutely. "I'm going to call right now."

"Wait!" Elizabeth called, her face suddenly lighting up. She pointed across the street. "Denise just came out!"

Winston rushed around to the front of the Jeep and heaved a deep sigh. Denise walked out alone, looking a little rumpled but in good shape. She smiled at them quickly, then gave a discreet thumbs-up before continuing up the sidewalk toward the residential area.

"Looks like the plan is in motion,"

Elizabeth said, getting out of the Jeep. "I told you everything would be all right."

Winston exhaled loudly, hardly realizing that he'd been holding his breath the entire time. *Denise is going to be OK,* he told himself, resisting the overpowering urge to run across the street and sweep her up in his arms. *She's going to be OK.*

"You'd better call," Elizabeth said, poking Winston in the ribs. While she seemed relieved that Denise was finally out of the bar, deep worry lines continued to crease her brow. "Give me a thumbs-up when you get through to the detectives."

Winston jogged down the sidewalk toward the phone. Relief was almost immediately over-shadowed with a new sense of urgency. With trembling hands he picked up the receiver and balanced it on his shoulder while he fed the coins through the slot. He quickly punched the number into the keypad and waited for the dial tone.

Nothing.

Come on . . . Denise was already past the parking lot, but Jackson was still in the bar. After a few seconds of silence Winston yanked on the coin return lever and tried again. Dead silence. He looked down the street to where Elizabeth stood waiting for his signal. *Come on, you stupid phone.* Winston smacked the side of it a few times with his fist, but still there was no dial tone.

It was broken.

"I can't believe this!" he shouted into the dark night air. After all the careful planning they had done, it was all going to fall apart because he had overlooked one crucial detail—he hadn't checked the phone. Now everything was going wrong.

Elizabeth held her hands up in the air, as if to ask what was going on. Denise was well past the clusters of trees and was heading toward the residential area. He jogged back to the Jeep.

"The phone doesn't work!" Winston felt his lungs collapsing, squeezing out every last bit of air. "Jackson's going to be out here any second," he wheezed.

A look of sheer terror froze on Elizabeth's face. "We have to keep him away from her!" she cried.

In a split second Elizabeth and Winston spun around and ran toward the bar.

Denise rubbed her cold arms, feeling the chilly night breeze blow right through her flimsy clothes. The alcohol made her feel heady, and her limbs were like weights, dragging her down. She continued walking on without looking back, just like Winston had said. So far there was no sign of Jackson.

The oily smell of Squid's vest hung like a cloud around her. *I thought I'd never get away from that creep*, she thought, listening to the crisp *clip-clop* of her high heels echoing through the desolate neighborhood. While Squid's furry arms were snaked around her waist, Denise had entertained notions of violence to get away from him. But before she had a chance to hit him with a well-placed knee, Jackson had walked up to the two of them and told Squid to leave her alone.

"What did you say to me?" Squid had growled, holding Denise even tighter.

Jackson had fixed Squid with a demonic stare. "I *said,* get your filthy paws off her. *Now.*"

Denise thought the two men were going to attack each other like wild dogs, but Jackson reached for something near his hip, and Squid suddenly backed off. Not sticking around to find out what it was that scared Squid, Denise had wrenched herself from his strong grip and headed for the door.

Where is Jackson? Denise folded her jittery arms across her chest, walking by a low iron fence that separated someone's grassy lawn from the paved sidewalk. She had assumed that Jackson had stood up for her so that he could have her all to himself. She thought he'd follow her the second she walked out of the bar. Denise halted for a moment and listened. Everything was still. The porch light from a nearby house cast an eerie glow on the sidewalk.

Heart pounding, Denise went against

Winston's orders and turned around, looking back at the path she had taken. Jackson was nowhere in sight.

Maybe I left too fast. Deep in the residential area, there was no way Jackson would try anything here with so much light and so many witnesses. *I've gone too far,* Denise thought, chewing nervously on her bottom lip. *I probably should walk back a little ways.* With a sigh of resolution she turned and headed back toward the parking lot.

Chapter Sixteen

Winston stormed into the bar and squinted in the odd green light. His eyes bounced from one beer drinker to the next. "I don't see him."

"He couldn't have gone far," Elizabeth answered between heavy breaths. Her head moved from side to side as she scanned the room. "We didn't see him go out the front door."

"Maybe he's in the men's room," Winston reasoned. The base of his spine tingled with new hope. "I'll check it out. Go ask the bartender if you can use the phone, then call the police station. Denise is still out there by herself—we don't have a lot of time."

Elizabeth nodded silently, then made her way across the room. Heads turned and conversations stopped as she walked by. "Well, looky here," shouted an overweight guy who was sitting on the pool table. "This must be our lucky night!"

Winston felt a sickening feeling in the pit of his stomach. *So this is what Denise had to deal with,* he thought with disgust. It was a wonder that she'd made it out of the bar at all.

Creeping along the back wall so no one would see him, Winston crawled around beer-soaked tables and chairs that were tipped over on their sides. He silently squeezed by a smoky poker game near the back of the bar. Every step he took was careful and deliberate as he tried not to draw attention to himself like he had at Gangbusters. Despite his caution Winston had the sneaking suspicion that even if he'd stood on a table and announced that he was there, no one would notice. They were all too busy drooling over Elizabeth.

"Come here, sweetie—I want to give you a kiss!" someone shouted from the bar.

Winston did a quick double check of the rowdy crowd from the pool table to the juke-box, but the killer was still nowhere in sight. He turned around the corner near the men's room, praying that Jackson was there but not having a clue what to do or say once he came face-to-face with him. With trembling fingers Winston grabbed the doorknob.

It turned easily. Taking a step back, Winston held his breath as the door creaked open, revealing an empty rest room. The one window in the room was up high and too narrow for even a child to fit through. There was no way Jackson could have crawled out.

Where did you go, you slimeball? Winston kicked the wall with the heel of his sneaker. Every nerve in his body was on edge as he stormed out the men's-room door. Just as Winston was about to turn the Lizard Lounge upside down, he spotted a glowing red exit sign a few feet away from the bathroom. It was then that Winston's last flicker of hope was snuffed out like a campfire in a rainstorm.

The door was open a crack. *Jackson went out the back way.* The realization hit Winston with a numbing fear that rocked him like a mortar shell. While Winston and Elizabeth were looking for Jackson in the bar, he was already long gone. Terror seared Winston's stomach like a branding iron. *The killer's probably already reached Denise by now.*

"May I help you, Angel Face?" the bartender asked.

Placing her hands on her hips and hardening her features, Elizabeth put on a tough exterior, even though her insides were turning to jelly. "I need to use your phone," she said roughly, mustering up as much attitude as she could find.

The bartender leaned forward on his elbows,

smiling slyly as if she'd just slipped him a pickup line. "Is that so, pretty lady?"

Elizabeth nervously checked the room a second time—still there was no sign of Jackson. *Where is he? Did he leave the bar without us noticing?* Elizabeth battled against the paralyzing fear that was creeping into her consciousness. "Yes—it's a matter of life and death."

"Ooooo—sounds serious." He pulled a black phone from under the bar and placed it on the counter.

Quickly Elizabeth reached for the phone, but just as her fingers grazed the receiver the bartender snatched it back again. "You can use it, but it'll cost you."

She reached into her pocket and laid a ten-dollar bill on the table. "It's all I have."

The bartender looked down at the money and laughed. "That wasn't exactly what I had in mind," he said, baring his rotten teeth. "I was thinking you could come over here and give me a little kiss."

"Drop dead," Elizabeth said bitingly.

"That little girl's a feisty one," the fat guy with the pool cue said. "I think you'd better teach her some manners, Teddy."

The bartender put the phone back under the counter. "Looks like you've just lost your calling privileges, little girl, but if you're real nice to me, maybe I'll give you a chance to get them back."

Elizabeth's fear was suddenly eclipsed by an explosive burst of fury. *What makes this loser think he can talk to me that way?* She bit the insides of her cheeks and swallowed the acerbic comments she was so ready to hurl at the bartender. There was no time to tell him what a jerk he was—she had to find Winston so they could get the police. If it wasn't already too late.

Turning around, Elizabeth suddenly found herself standing inches from a hulking biker. He was staring down at her with a creepy grin on his face.

"Do you need to go somewhere, cutie?" the biker said, pointing to the key ring clipped to his leather pants. "My Harley's parked out front—I'll take you anywhere you want to go."

The corners of Elizabeth's mouth sank in a deep frown as she shot him a look of disgust. "Buzz off!"

A group of men gathered around the two of them, laughing. Elizabeth tried to break through the menacing circle, but the biker snaked a furry arm around her waist and pulled her back.

"Get your hands off me, bozo!" Elizabeth screamed, pummeling his iron chest with her fists.

Still smiling, the biker just looked down at Elizabeth, who was struggling futilely like a housefly caught in a spiderweb. "Let me know when it's supposed to hurt," he said, snickering at her weak punches.

Elizabeth's face grew hot as she wrestled against his grip. The biker's thick fingers were digging deep into her ribs.

"Let her go!" shouted a voice from behind.

Elizabeth turned her head to see Winston coming at them, his lips quivering and pale. His large brown eyes were filled with fear.

The biker, still keeping his effortless hold on Elizabeth, sneered at Winston. "What did you just say to me, *punk?*"

"I *said*, let her go—*now*." Winston drew himself up to his full height, which still only reached about the middle of the biker's chest.

"You want me to let her go?"

Winston's eyes narrowed. "Don't make me repeat myself."

A hush fell over the crowd. To Elizabeth's surprise, the biker slowly released his grip. She hopped back a few steps, out of reach, and stood near Winston.

Winston's jaw fell open slightly. He seemed more surprised than Elizabeth that his bravado actually worked. "Are you all right?" he asked, pulling her to the side.

"I'm fine," Elizabeth said, rubbing the sore spot where the biker's fingers had dug into her. "Did you find Jackson?"

Chapter Seventeen

I have to find Denise. . . . The words turned over and over again in Winston's mind with desperate urgency. Gripping the handlebars in his fists, he felt the motorcycle engine thundering beneath him. He roared up the street, searching the area for any sign of Denise. The streets were deserted, with alternating patches of inky shadows and dim pools of light.

"Denise!" Winston screamed into the pitch-black sky, knowing his voice couldn't be carried above the noise of the bike. He revved the engine a few times. House lights came on all over the dark residential area. Winston didn't care if he woke up everyone in the entire neighborhood—maybe someone would see Denise.

What was that? Out of the corner of his eye Winston swore he saw some movement near a spot dense with trees. It had only been a split-second glint in the round handlebar mirror, hardly anything that would have normally caught his attention. But an inner voice told Winston it was something he couldn't ignore. *You have to go there,* it said. *It could be her.*

Winston revved the motorcycle engine again. The wind burned against his swollen face as he did a U-turn in the middle of the street. He swung around and headed back toward the cluster of trees. *If anything happens to her, I'll never forgive myself.*

He cut the loud engine and knew immediately that his instincts had been right. A few yards away muffled cries were rising up from behind the trees.

Winston's blood ran cold.

"Get away from her!" Winston yelled, hurtling over a low row of hedge. He shoved back tree branches and sprinted around the twisting roots until he came upon the spot where the struggle was taking place. Denise was on the ground, lying on her back, the blond wig off her head but still connected by a strand of hair. Jackson was standing over her, dragging her brutally by the ankles toward a thicker growth of trees.

"Help!" Denise cried, her voice cracking in terror.

"Shut up!" Jackson shouted back.

Suddenly Winston could feel the adrenaline taking over his body, running through his veins. He pounced onto Jackson's back and wrapped his arms around his torso like an iron belt, immobilizing his arms. But Jackson still held firm to Denise.

"Let go of her!" Winston shouted in the killer's ear.

"Winston!" Denise cried in fright as she watched them struggle.

Jackson finally dropped Denise's ankles and started to spin in circles, fighting to break from Winston's grip.

"Denise—get away!" Winston yelled. The muscles in his arms burned under the strain. He couldn't hold on much longer.

Denise rolled to the side, then scurried out of harm's way. "Winston—watch out!"

But the advice came too late. Jackson had slammed backward against one of the big trees, pinning Winston against it. The impact sent a shattering pain through every fiber of his body. Winston's arms automatically let go, the jagged tree bark digging into the flesh of his back as he dropped to the ground.

Jackson's upper lip curled into an evil sneer as he approached him. Winston felt Jackson deliver a powerful kick to his ribs with the pointed toe of one of his cowboy boots. As Winston's body contorted with excruciating pain, Jackson squatted next to him and looked into his eyes. "Looks like I got me two for the price of one tonight."

"You stay away from him!" Denise's eyes were ablaze. She had started to run toward the road for help when Jackson drew his hunting knife and held it up for her to see. Denise stopped dead in her tracks. Winston felt the cold edge of a six-inch steel blade against his throat.

"No one's going anywhere," Jackson said.

"I still don't quite follow what this is all about," Detective Martin said as he pulled the police car out of the parking lot. "You three were making up your own sting operation?"

Reese, who was sitting on the passenger's side, eyed Elizabeth with suspicion. "I don't know about this, Martin—what if they're just setting us up?"

"Why would I do that?" Elizabeth shouted, pressing her face against the cage that divided the back of the police car from the front. "I was one of the people he attacked, remember?"

Reese continued talking to Martin, as if Elizabeth weren't there. "Egbert could've brainwashed her into thinking it was Jackson Lowe who did it."

"It *was* Jackson Lowe," Elizabeth snapped. "And I do have a brain of my own, *thank you very much*."

"There's no harm in checking the story out," Martin said, turning the car onto the main drag. "If this is a setup, we'll just pick up Egbert a little earlier than we planned."

Reese turned around and glared at Elizabeth. "If you're making this up, I'm going to make sure we get you both for obstruction of justice."

Elizabeth ignored him and looked out the window. The car seemed to be moving at a snail's pace, as if they were out on a Sunday drive instead of trying to stop a killer. She smacked the cage impatiently. "Can't we speed this up a little? Someone's life is in danger," she cried. "Or maybe you two don't care if more blood is spilled."

Martin and Reese exchanged looks, then the detective put his foot on the gas. His eyes met Elizabeth's in the rearview mirror. "Where did you say we'd find Winston?"

"At the Lizard Lounge. He was out cold when I left him," she answered, glad they were finally taking her seriously. "As soon as we get him out of there we have to find Denise. There's a good chance Jackson's going to follow her." A shiver of dread passed ran down the middle of her back. "If he hasn't already."

The detectives parked the squad car outside the bar. Elizabeth unbuckled her seat belt and opened the back door.

"You're staying here," Reese muttered, slamming the door closed again.

Elizabeth rolled the window down a crack. "I want to go with you. I know where Winston is."

"You're staying right here until we get back," Reese said. His sandy eyebrows knitted in a mistrusting way. "Don't try anything."

Elizabeth sighed in exasperation. *I love being treated like a criminal when I haven't even done anything wrong,* she thought bitterly. The detectives walked into the bar, taking their time, as if they were going in for a drink instead of looking for a serial killer. Elizabeth gnawed anxiously on her fingernails, wishing she'd gone to look for Denise herself.

Less than a minute later they returned—without Winston.

Martin opened the car door. "He's not in there."

"What?" Elizabeth shook her head. Winston was out cold when she left him. What could have happened?

"I told you I had a bad feeling about this," Reese muttered, getting back into the squad car. "The guys in the bar said Winston smashed someone in the face with a beer mug, then stole his Harley."

Way to go, Winston, Elizabeth thought as they pulled back out onto the road.

"Wait a second," Martin said suddenly,

pointing at something up ahead. "Isn't that the bike right there?"

Elizabeth looked out the windshield and spotted the Harley lying on its side in the middle of the road, about a hundred yards ahead.

"Looks like Egbert didn't make it too far," Reese said.

Elizabeth's heart plummeted with a sickening thud.

"Let him go!" Denise sobbed, staring into Jackson's crazed eyes. The killer grabbed Winston by the hair and yanked his head back, pressing the sharp blade against his throat. A razor-thin line of crimson blood appeared on Winston's skin.

Jackson ignored her, putting the tip of the blade under Winston's ear. The green rattlesnake on his forearm quivered as he expertly gripped the blade in his hand. Winston cried out, his sobs anticipating certain death.

The terror was building in her mind, threatening her sanity. She watched as Jackson sank the blade a little deeper into Winston's skin, and he howled in pain. In the blink of an eye he could be out of her life forever.

I can't live without you, Winston.

In a last, desperate effort Denise fell to her knees. "Please—please don't kill him; let him go!" she begged. "Let him go!"

Jackson paused, looking down at Denise. The sharp blade flickered in the moonlight. "Are you sorry for what you've done?"

Denise had no idea what he was referring to, but she'd say anything if it meant saving Winston. "I'm so sorry!" she wailed, throwing herself at his feet. "I'll never do it again, I promise!"

"Of course you'll do it again," Jackson said, looking straight at her. He dropped the knife at his side but continued to hold Winston by the hair. "You won't be able to help yourself."

"I don't want to do that anymore," Denise argued blindly, heavy sobs rising in her chest. "I don't want to be that way anymore."

Jackson smiled. "Do you want me to help you change?"

"I'll do anything to change," Denise said, cowering in fright.

"There's only one thing that can free you." He held up the knife. A drop of Winston's blood trickled down the blade.

Denise bit the inside of her cheeks to keep from screaming. She stared up at Jackson as bravely as she could, her body on the verge of collapse. Time was running out for both of them. Winston looked at her, his eyes glassy and empty, already seeming to accept his fate.

Don't give up on me now, Winston.

Jackson put the blade against Winston's neck again. Denise sat up and leaned back her head, offering up her pale, slender neck as a sacrifice. "You should take me instead."

Jackson stared at her throat. He was mesmerized by it, his hard eyes transfixed. With his free hand he reached out and followed the long curve of it with his fingers, from her chin down to her collarbone.

"Please let him go," Denise appealed to Jackson. "Kill me instead."

Jackson laughed loudly, pulling away his hand. "Don't you worry, little darling, you'll get your wish. As soon as I'm done with him, you're next."

Just beyond the trees she caught a glimpse of a police car driving by. It slowed down as it approached. Denise wanted desperately to scream out, but a wrong move could prove fatal for either one of them.

Denise stood up and faced Jackson. "I want to die first."

Winston struggled a little, the knife cutting into him. "Don't, Denise—just stay out of this."

The police car stopped and two detectives stealthily slipped out of the car and walked up and down the sidewalk. No one but Denise knew they were there. *We're too deep into the thicket,* she thought. *They're never going to be able to see us.*

Denise swallowed hard, putting her hand

over Jackson's and closing her fingers around the handle of the knife. She stared into his cold eyes and slowly pulled the blade away from Winston's neck. Then, with her hand still around Jackson's, Denise put the blade up to her own throat.

"Denise, don't—" Winston whimpered.

"You shut up!" Jackson yelled, yanking Winston's head back even farther.

Jackson's voice must have carried to the road because Denise saw the detectives look up suddenly. The younger one drew his gun, hurrying over silently and creeping up behind Jackson.

Denise pretended not to notice the detective as he inched closer. *It's almost over,* she thought tensely. "I want to die first," she repeated, holding Jackson's chilly gaze.

"All right, angel," Jackson said, running the knifepoint along her cheek. "Whatever you want."

Detective Reese stepped forward and pressed the barrel of his gun against the back of Jackson's head. "Drop the knife or I'll shoot."

Jackson froze, his eyes turning sad and hollow as he raised his hands in the air. The knife tumbled to the ground.

Winston took Denise in his arms and held her closer than he ever had before. *It's over,* he

272

thought with a deep sigh, his body still trembling uncontrollably. *It's finally over.*

"Are you all right?" he asked, his finger tracing the thin red scratch Jackson had made across her cheek.

"I'm fine," Denise answered, somehow managing a smile. Gently she reached up and touched the side of his swollen face and the cut on his neck. "Are you OK? You don't look so hot."

"I'll be all right." Winston sighed. Denise pressed her cheek against his chest, making him nearly melt with happiness. "As long as you're with me, I'll be fine."

The backup squad cars pulled up, with their flashing blue lights and screaming sirens. Winston carefully touched the tip of Denise's chin and tilted her face up toward his. "Thank you so much for what you did," he said, looking into her eyes. "I know I don't deserve it."

Denise smiled sheepishly. "You're right— you don't deserve it."

Winston lowered his head, resting his forehead against hers. "So why did you risk your life for me?"

"Unfortunately I have a problem—I'm madly in love with you," Denise teased.

Winston suppressed a smile. "It sounds serious. When the ambulance gets here, maybe you should have the paramedics check you out."

"I have a better idea," Denise said coyly, the blue lights flashing behind her. Moving closer, she wrapped her arms around Winston's neck and kissed him passionately.

Their embrace was interrupted by a piercing shout. "You've got the wrong man!" Jackson screamed as Detective Martin put the cuffs on him. Detective Reese dragged the killer away and shoved him into the back of the car.

Winston looked over to see the chief homicide detective coming toward him. For the first time the sight of Detective Martin didn't fill him with dread.

"You mean we *had* the wrong man," Martin corrected Jackson's rantings. He held his hand out to Winston. "It was a very stupid thing you did tonight. Congratulations—you're lucky it worked."

Winston shook the detective's hand firmly. "I didn't have much of a choice, sir."

Reese slammed the door to the squad car and strolled over to where they were standing. "Good job, Egbert. We could probably use a guy like you on the force." He smiled faintly and shook Winston's hand.

"No, thanks," Winston answered. "I think I've had enough excitement for a long time."

The detectives went back to the car and

radioed for an ambulance and police backup. Elizabeth ran over to them with arms outstretched and hugged both Denise and Winston. "I'm so glad you both are all right," she said.

Winston wrapped his arm around her shoulders. "Thanks for your help, Liz."

Elizabeth's lips twisted into a sly smile. "Now that this is all over, what do you say we go to the Lizard Lounge and celebrate?"

Chapter Eighteen

A few weeks later Winston was sitting across from Denise as they ate breakfast in the cafeteria. He hardly touched his pancakes, too distracted by the gentle morning sun casting a glow on Denise's sweet face. All he could do was sit and watch her, perfectly content.

Denise looked up from the omelette that she was digging into hungrily. "What's wrong, Winnie?"

Winston smiled lazily, pushing aside his plate. "I was just thinking about how lucky I am."

"Lucky?"

"You know," he said, looking into her eyes, "that my life has almost returned to normal. I never thought it could go back to the way it was before."

"It's not exactly back to normal," she said,

taking a bite of toast. "You lost your job."

"I know," Winston answered. He wasn't sad about it—it would have been far too difficult to face Dean Franklin after everything that had happened. Shortly after Jackson's arrest Winston told the dean the entire story—he thought he deserved to know exactly why Amanda had been murdered. Dean Franklin took it better than Winston thought he would, thanking him for telling the truth. The last Winston had heard, the dean had decided to take a year off to get his life back in order.

"I wasn't just talking about the job, though," Winston continued. "I was thinking how lucky I am that we're still together."

Denise wiped the corners of her mouth with her napkin. "But it's still not exactly like it was before. It's going to take a while to build back trust."

Winston nodded. "I'm just grateful you're giving me a second chance."

Elizabeth suddenly burst through the cafeteria door and dropped the morning newspaper right in the middle of the table. "Check out the headline," she said, falling into the seat next to Winston.

Winston read the headline aloud. "'Sweet Valley Serial Killer Sentenced to Life in Prison.' I thought I'd never see the day."

"I guess it's finally over," Elizabeth said.

"I'm definitely going to sleep better knowing that Jackson Lowe will spend the rest of his life behind bars."

Denise leaned across the table and kissed Winston lightly on the lips. "Congratulations, Winnie. You did it."

"*We* did it," he corrected.

"We sure did." Denise smiled, but then her face grew serious. "Don't you *ever* cheat on me again."

"Don't worry," Winston said solemnly. "I've definitely learned my lesson."

"What's that?" Denise asked.

Winston reached across the table for Denise's hand. "That there's no one else I'd rather be with than you."

SIGN UP FOR THE SWEET VALLEY HIGH® FAN CLUB!

Hey, girls! Get all the gossip on Sweet Valley High's® most popular teenagers when you join our fantastic Fan Club! As a member, you'll get all of this really cool stuff:

- Membership Card with your own personal Fan Club ID number
- A Sweet Valley High® Secret Treasure Box
- Sweet Valley High® Stationery
- Official Fan Club Pencil (for secret note writing!)
- Three Bookmarks
- A "Members Only" Door Hanger
- Two Skeins of J. & P. Coats® Embroidery Floss with flower barrette instruction leaflet
- Two editions of *The Oracle* newsletter
- Plus exclusive Sweet Valley High® product offers, special savings, contests, and much more!

- -

Be the first to find out what Jessica & Elizabeth Wakefield are up to by joining the Sweet Valley High® Fan Club for the one-year membership fee of only $6.25 each for U.S. residents, $8.25 for Canadian residents (U.S. currency). Includes shipping & handling.

Send a check or money order (do not send cash) made payable to "Sweet Valley High® Fan Club" along with this form to:

SWEET VALLEY HIGH® FAN CLUB, BOX 3919-B, SCHAUMBURG, IL 60168-3919

NAME_____
(Please print clearly)

ADDRESS_____

CITY_____ STATE _____ ZIP_____
(Required)

AGE_____ BIRTHDAY_____ /_____ /_____

Offer good while supplies last. Allow 6-8 weeks after check clearance for delivery. Addresses without ZIP codes cannot be honored. Offer good in USA & Canada only. Void where prohibited by law.
©1993 by Francine Pascal   LCI-1383-123